A Gentle Nudge

A Gentle Nudge

Mason Bushell

Bridge House

British Library Cataloguing in Publication Data
A Record of this Publication is available from the British
Library

ISBN 978-1-914199-42-4

This edition published 2023 by Bridge House Publishing
Manchester, England

Contents

A Chance Encounter with Love

The clouds were gathering beyond the silvery surf this afternoon. Glen and his dog Willard always walked the clifftop path each day. At thirty, Glen had a hole in his heart. He'd felt love for a girl just once as a teenager. He failed to make the connection he felt in his heart with her though. Maybe that was why fourteen years later, love had never blossomed again.

Those thoughts left him wistful on days like today. He felt as though love would never come now, he was too old for such a thing – wasn't he?

"Come away from the edge, Willard!" he called to the brown-and-white English Pointer.

Willard returned a wag of his thin tail and obeyed.

"Good, lad." Glen gazed ahead, watching a lady in a burgundy and black running vest and shorts, jogging toward him. Even from three-hundred-yards, he could tell her titian hair was the same shade and ponytailed just as Remy's always was at school.

Willard looked to the moody skies and barked.

"I agree, a storm's brewing up there." Glen cast his eyes over the scudding clouds. "Time to get h—"

Lightning tore open the darkened skies. The thunder which followed was like a monstrous bowling ball crashing down the alley. There was something more. As the rain began to deluge the cliff face, Glen heard a terrified scream.

Willard howled and ran to his master.

Glen couldn't see the runner anywhere; she'd gone. Realising why, he burst into a run. Sideways rain whipped across the clifftop as the squall storm arrived in a fury.

The thunder rolled with such intensity it made man and dog cower as they sprinted through the torrential downpour.

Both Glen and Willard were soaked in seconds but pushed on regardless.

The clifftop used to have safety railing. Erosion had sent many of the bars to the beach almost a hundred feet below. Even now the rains were causing more of the clay to slide and fall from the face.

Glen ran to where he thought the runner had been before the lightning struck. He forced his eyes open against the wind and rain and started searching for her. "Lady! Where are you?"

Willard had gone on further; he pawed at the ground and barked.

"I'm here!" she cried from below him.

"Good, boy!" Glen ran to him and scratched his soggy ears for a moment. There was one upright post of the old railing left here. He wrapped the dog's lead around it and secured it to his belt. "Don't move!" he threatened the post as he dropped to his belly and leaned over the edge.

The beach seemed to rise toward him. There was a lot of rock down there; a fall would almost certainly be fatal.

The lady screamed.

Glen snapped back to reality, threw out a hand and caught her about the wrist as the cliff fell away beneath her. "Kick your feet in. Get a grip!" he urged while fighting not to let her slip through his wet hand as the storm raged on.

"Help me!" she cried scrabbling helplessly.

"Kick the wall and get a foot in!" Glen yelled over another deep rumble of thunder.

She did and this time she made a solid purchase on the clay wall. As she held on she looked straight into her rescuer's face.

Glen felt like he'd been shot by the lightning. Rainwater flooded his eyes leaving his vision blurred, a sensation which only added to his heart pounding madly in his chest.

He flashed back to an earlier time on the school playing field; wishing she would notice him, yearning to kiss her. Those amber eyes were still the same. His soul told him this was her. "Remy?"

"I'm slipping!" she cried.

"No, you're not!" Glen reached down as far as he could and latched his free hand under her arm. "Get up her-argh!" he roared as he forced his muscles to lift her.

Willard took hold of his belt and hauled on him as well.

"Good boy, Willard!" Glen gritted his teeth. "Come on!"

Inch by inch, the lady was pulled through torrents of water and mud until she was lying on the cliff top, exhausted but alive.

Glen collapsed beside her with Willard licking his face. Despite the ordeal, he was smiling at the chance encounter. Above him, a golden light had come over the storm clouds. Sun began to split through the darkness. Glen felt fingers take his hand and hold tight.

"You saved me," she said.

"You near gave me a heart attack disappearing in front of me like that!" he replied still sucking in deep breaths. "I'm glad you're alive."

"Me too! I'm a little wet and dirty, but I'll be fine thanks to you – Glen."

Glen rolled to face her. "Remy, it is you."

She nodded. "I remember you. Always in the background smiling toward me but never having the courage to speak to me."

"Yup, that was cowardly me," Glen admitted.

"Then I was a coward too. I couldn't bring myself to speak to you either. I was scared, I didn't know what to do." She giggled. "Silly kids, huh!"

"Just a bit. What now?" Glen asked. All these years later he still didn't know what to do.

9

"Look." Remi accepted a lick from Willard and pointed to the sky. A beautiful rainbow spanned the cliff top, splitting the ominous clouds into the most mesmerising prism of colour and beauty.

"Oh, that's magic!" Glen grinned having rolled on to his back again.

"It's more than that. It's the sign I've been waiting for."

"I don't understand."

"When the sky is turned aglow by the colours of a magnificent rainbow. Your soulmate will be there to take your hand and hold your heart forevermore." Remy said.

"That's beautiful." Glen frowned as she beamed toward him. He felt sure he'd missed something.

"A fortune-teller told me that when I was twenty-five. I never believed in such things until you rescued me by taking my hand and then the sky gave us this magical rainbow." Remy sat up and looked into his eyes.

Glen returned the look. "I'd be happy to hold your hand and take care of your heart forever, Remy."

Remy reached forward and brushed her cheek against his as she kissed him.

For the second time in five minutes, Glen felt struck by the lightning. Her energy filled every cell in his body with euphoria.

Willard had seen enough; he began kissing both of them with enormous doggy licks.

"Pah! You know, Glen. If we're going to kiss more often – and I hope we are – we're going to need different arrangements for this guy!" Remy poked the dog in the nose, laughed and hugged him and Glen together.

Glen just looked at the rainbow and grinned. "Thank you, Mother Nature."

Ben's Birds

"Such a strange, speckled chest. Whatever sort of bird could that be?" Ben exchanged his binoculars for his camera. In his twenties, he was young for a twitcher. His grandmother had instilled a love of birds and wildlife in him at a young age. Now, he loved nothing more than to be within nature; listening for and tracking elusive birds he hadn't seen yet.

He zoomed into the sycamore tree and clicked off a couple of shots. "Hmm, your speckles are wrong for a fieldfare. You have no red areas, so you're not redwing. What are you?" Ben crept closer, clicking off more shots as he edged along the trail.

The bird didn't linger long. It gave a musical chirp and fluttered to a nearby oak tree.

Ben followed, watching it chase off blackbirds. He'd become tunnel-visioned – blinded by intrigue at the mystery bird. He was so focused on the camera's viewfinder that he'd lost his bearings. He'd walked from the wood-chipping trail. An acorn skipping beneath his feet sent him tumbling. Crying out, he felt his shoulder, head and knees all slamming into the ground as he bounced down the hillside. He struck trees and crashed through bushes until he came to a stop on a lower trail.

"Oh, you poor thing! Are you okay?" asked a melodious, friendly voice before the dust even settled.

Ben lay on his chest gasping for breath – hurting all over. "Argh! That was a rough ride!" He tried to roll but felt a hand laid across his shoulder, preventing him.

"Just take it easy for a moment. We need to check be sure you're okay before you move."

Ben forced himself on to his side and felt liquid running down his face. That was all he needed. He was bleeding. Crouching beside him, was a young lady in a cute khaki dress and brown leather cowboy boots. She had her tawny hair pulled back with a 90s' style headband which suited her soft round features. "Thank you for stopping to help me," he managed before breaking into a coughing fit.

"That's okay. I'm Melissa." She smiled through her concern. "Do you think you've broken anything?"

"I'm, Ben. Ahh... Erm?" Feeling no neck and spinal pain, he pulled himself into a sitting position. Pain flared in his hip and shoulder but nothing seemed broken. "Yowie! I think I nearly broke my arse and shoulder, but I'll be okay!"

"That's a good thing. You do have a cut to your left temple though." Melissa reached into her handbag and withdrew some tissues. With a gentle hand, she began to stem the bleeding. "It might be a good idea to get you to the ranger's station and have a paramedic look you over. If not I can call an ambulance from here."

"I'm sure I can walk. I think I'll see how I feel when I get to the station and call paramedics there if I need them." Ben reached for his camera and binoculars. Mercifully, other than a couple of scrapes they seemed undamaged.

Melissa looked between the gadgets and Ben. "You weren't up there spying on me, were you?"

Ben felt his heart thump at the accusation. "No! No, I... I'm a twitcher. I was following a bird I hadn't seen before when I fell down the hillside, that's all."

"Really?" Melissa giggled, yet remained suspicious. "Prove it."

Ben swiftly pulled-up his latest picture and handed her camera. "See, it's definitely in the thrush family but I'm not sure what is." He explained while watching her looking at the screen and thumbing through a few images.

"Wow, Ben. These are great photographs of a mistle thrush." Melissa returned the camera. "You should print those and put them in a lovely frame."

"Thanks, that's a good idea." Ben allowed her to help him stand. It was then for the first time as she held him, that he smelled her cherry and vanilla perfume. The scent ignited something within him he'd never encountered before. A desire to be with her, a passion to love her, he realised.

"I'd be honoured to have one of your pictures." Melissa smiled at him as they set off along the track. This one bordered a pretty lake which was home to a wide variety of waterfowl, fish, insects and other wildlife. Most notable were the large flock of mute swans.

"Then we'll arrange that," Ben promised. "How did you know what the bird was?"

"You see the willow bench over there. The obituary written on the back belongs to my grandmother. She brought me here every weekend as I grew up. She taught me all about the birds and wildlife here. Now, I often walk here alone just to be near her." Melissa paused to wipe her eyes. "You see, I know her spirit still roams here in her favourite place to be."

"That's a sweet story. My grandmother made me a bird lover too. Seems we have a few things in common." Ben approached the bench and read the inscription on its black plaque. "It's a pleasure to meet you, Catherine. I must say you have a wonderful granddaughter who is taking good care of me. I'll come and say 'hi' when I pass by in future. Until then have a lovely day," he said as if Melissa's grandmother was sitting on the bench.

Melissa smiled through watery eyes when he returned to her. "That was so thoughtful of you, Ben. Thank you."

Ben nodded as they set off again. The two chatted a little more, sharing stories and getting to know each other. They paused to point out woodpeckers, nuthatches and a flock of greenfinches. Many of which Ben managed to capture with his camera.

"Want to know a secret?" Melissa said after a while.

It was Ben's turn to look suspicious now. "Sure?"

"I knew you weren't spying on me. I just needed an excuse to look at your pictures," Melissa said.

"Huh! Cheeky, devil. You could have just asked." Ben chuckled. All too soon they emerged from the nature reserve into the car park.

"We made it! How are you feeling?" Melissa asked.

"Once I've had a shower, I think I'll be okay. Thanks to you looking after me." Ben looked to his feet as nervousness took over.

"I'm glad you'll be okay."

"While there is one small problem."

"Really? What?" Melissa asked as they came to a stop behind a little green hatchback.

"Well, after spending such a lovely time walking back with you. I'm going to have to eat dinner alone tonight. Don't know how I can fix that, do you?" Ben looked hopeful.

Melissa blushed and swayed on her feet. "Are you asking me out on a date, mister?"

"Just to thank you for caring for me." Ben hoped he wasn't being pushy. Seeing her smile, he decided to risk more. "Maybe, we could meet here for a walk from time to time too."

"I'd like that. I've been alone for a fair while. It'd be lovely to have your company." Melissa moved in front of him and they shared a kiss which seemed to linger just long enough to mean more than "thank you".

As Ben left her to drive home, he felt he'd gotten very lucky. The fall hadn't resulted in serious injuries or a broken camera for that matter. He'd discovered a new bird for him and found a little love in the process. What could be luckier than that?

Benny and the New Years' Fireworks

Benny the German Shepherd hated New Year. He knew it was coming tonight and he was dreading it. The first clue was that funny plastic fir tree with the sparkly balls; it was always an early warning before the explosions began. He never could understand why he got yelled at for playing with those hanging balls. They were for playing with, weren't they?

He'd eaten a big bowl of delicious roast turkey six days ago, so now it was time for the blasted fireworks to start thundering and banging all over the sky. Benny lay in his blanket-covered cage with his paws over his head. Those fireworks scared him so much. He knew his master and mistress loved them; they'd been excited to go and celebrate all day. That was why Benny lay all alone, shaking in his cage.

The fireworks began way before midnight; they always did. To the German Shepherd, it was like being in a warzone, with the flashes through the windows and grenade-like explosions that left him trembling with an urge to burrow into the earth and hide. Through the cacophonous tumult, he heard another sound. A scream, a human cry for help.

Benny stood and left his cage with a shake of his black and tan fur. The room shook with a deafening bang, a rocket detonating over the house. Benny whimpered and padded out of the lounge, his claws clicking over the tiles as he entered the kitchen. His ears were erect and swivelling, his eyes wide and looking all about. The screamer was in trouble, he could still hear her. He could hear another firework shrieking out in the darkness too.

"*Help me!*" The voice was muffled and distant.

Benny howled and pawed at the locked back door.

"Please help!"

15

Benny tilted his head, thinking, then he was running. He leapt upon a dining chair and climbed onto the table. The festive table cloth shot away from beneath him, spilling the last two crackers and a small Christmas tree ornament to the floor with some cutlery. With a nimble bounce, he jumped on to the kitchen work surface and walked around to the window.

"Help me!"

The call was much louder to Benny now he was near the open window. Benny knew that voice. The owner gave him treats and lots of hugs when she came home at three-thirty most afternoons. He reached with his wet nose and pushed the window open wider still. A rocket detonating in a flash of red sparks just beyond the window caused him to whimper and back away. He heard the female cry again and shook himself. Leaping through the open window, his claws scrabbled and clattered on the glass, then he was out in the chilly air and falling. He landed hard on the patio, yelped and raced under the nearest bush to avoid more screaming fireworks. Benny was a bundle of nerves, his eyes were wild, his tongue panting and dripping on to the earth, despite it being near freezing outside.

"Somebody, help!"

Benny peered out of the bush and looked toward the panicked voice. His neighbour's house was engulfed in flames and smoke. Benny leapt clear of the foliage, scaring the feral cat he'd befriended this winter. Ignoring the indignant hisses from the tabby, he streaked across the lawn. Around his home to the side-gate he went. Throwing his paws high, he balanced on the fence post and used his teeth to pop the latch off. Benny put on a doggy smile as the gate swung open; he'd seen his master do that trick. Down the driveway, he went. Almost at the road, he dropped flat, paws over his head as a rocket whipped into the sky and went bang like a crackling, roaring hellhound. Benny barked angrily at it, then remembered his friend next door. He ran the other way along the pavement and pawed at the first house door he came too. His urgent scraping and barking brought the grey-haired man out to see him.

"Hallo, Benny. Did you escape, old boy?" he asked while tickling him about the ears.

Benny shook his head, he grabbed the man's pyjama leg and dragged him outside. He gave a warning bark and raced away down the garden again. Stopping by the road, he indicated the smoke and fire with a nod of his furry head and another whining bark.

"Good boy, Benny. I see the fire." said the old man going for his phone.

Benny sprinted back along the path into the garden of the burning house. He was so filled with adrenaline and desire to help he was ignoring fireworks now. He saw no way into the house and so skirted a hedgehog on his way into the back garden. He'd poked his nose on hedgehogs before, and knew them a dangerous thing to step on.

"Benny, help me!" screamed the young lady.

Benny peered through the smoke and flames and saw her looking through the window above him. He also noticed the rear door was open. Ignoring the danger he gave a "woof!" and leapt inside. The acrid smoke caused his nose to wrinkle and his eyes to sting. He sneezed and growled at the pain it caused. The dog instinctively stayed low as he moved through the house. Reaching the stairs, he padded into thicker smoke. He could feel the heat now. Higher he went until he was on the fiery landing. He gave a tentative sniff and a howl as he realised the door marked "Emily" was ablaze – he could sense her panicking inside.

Benny turned his head from side to side, his mind searching for solutions. What had the humans done that he

17

could use to help Emily? His eyes fell upon the windowsill. A big vase of roses was on it, Benny leapt at the curtain and yanked on it with desperate growls and tugs. The rail broke with a nasty crack. Down it came spilling the vase. Water and roses cascaded over the flaming door, soaking the dog's head and the curtain. Benny shook himself and rammed the door with his head, throwing it open.

"Benny!" Emily's face was gaunt with fear and glistening with tears as she sat curled at the smoky window. Tendrils of smoke billowed around her leaving her coughing in the face of certain death if she didn't escape soon.

The dog raced to her with a welcome bark and a wag of his tail. He took hold of her nightdress and tugged it.

"Benny, the fire!"

Benny bounced on his hind legs and pulled her again. This time Emily nodded and followed him. The dog pushed her ahead of him as they plunged out of her room, through the flames and into the smoke. A ceiling beam crashed down in an explosion of flames. It thumped off the dogs broad back, slamming him to the carpet. Benny yelped and bounded free, his back smoking from the flames. He was injured, and could only limp downstairs. The dog whimpered through his pain, forcing his hip and back onward. He never stopped nudging and pushing his friend away from the danger. She hit the ground floor running and unlocked the front door. In an explosion of smoke, she burst onto the front lawn, with Benny limping out behind her. A thunderous explosion blew out the upper windows of the house showering them both in the glass. It was then the bright red and noisy fire engines blared into view and stopped.

Benny collapsed onto the lawn with Emily's shaking arms around him. He gave her a fond look while panting through his pain. He felt quite pleased with himself for rescuing her.

"Thank you for saving me, Benny sweetheart," she said in a tearful voice as she kissed his silky nose. Around her firefighters unslung hoses and began tackling the inferno.

"Woof!" he said as a tall fireman knelt before him and shook his paw.

"Well done, dog. You should be a firefighter," he said smoothing his silky head.

Benny licked his hand and blinked at the grey-haired gentleman from two doors down. He was close by on the pavement, having told the fireman of Benny's heroics.

In the days that followed Benny was hailed a hero in the papers. His burns and bruises would heal and his pile of ham bone rewards kept growing. A single stray rocket was put down as the cause of the blaze. Benny's face was put in a place of honour upon warnings about firework safety, warnings which appeared in every media around the world. Benny had become a heroic safety dog and Emily's best friend forever.

Bridge of Life

"Don't you dare come any closer!" Lily said over the rumble and swish of the traffic passing beneath the bridge.

"What? Why?" said Ned looking miffed in the orange light of the street lamp. As romantic dates went, spending the night on the motorway overpass bridge beneath the phone mast, had to be the weirdest. Unless this was where you met the love of your life, of course.

"I'll jump!" Lily set her chestnut hair free from its scrunchie. She smoothed the brown striped jumper and curled her back over the railing. The dizzying lights of the traffic now seemed to pass upside down beneath her.

"Please, Lily. Don't be silly!" Ned held out his hands. "Please, come away from the railing and let me hold you."

"No, stay away or I'll jump!" Lily leaned further back over the edge.

"Hey! Have you any idea of the upheaval you'll cause. All those innocent people in the cars will crash and may die. You will be dead and I'll be forced to jump off this bridge too," Ned said feeling sick with fear.

"Why would you jump?" Lily asked.

"Because I love you, silly. I don't have a reason to live unless it's with you." Ned offered her his hands again. "Now, please come back to me."

Lily rolled her back straight and smiled at him. Turning a strong cartwheel into a front flip, she landed in his arms with the gracefulness of the gymnast she was.

"Thank you, sweetheart," he said as they brushed noses and kissed.

"That was the sweetest thing anybody's ever said to me." Lily pressed her forehead against his absorbing his energy in a way that left her tingling. "I love you, Ned."

"Then why were you going to jump?" Ned asked as he

began to turn her in soft circles. Not even the roar of the lorry beneath them could break the spellbinding moment.

"I wasn't. I just wanted to see how you'd react." Lily grinned.

"Cheeky! Well, how'd I do?"

"A-star! You are the perfect romantic gentleman,"

The couple kissed and then he turned her back to him and held her tight. "I love how the cars shine a spotlight upon our souls. The stars above, the audience twinkling their approval of our love."

"Aww – the phone mast must be transmitting pictures of us surrounded in hearts to the world."

"Bloody hope not!" Ned turned her into a pirouette and bent her back to kiss her like the finale of a romantic dance.

She reached up and blocked the kiss with a finger on his nose. "Why?"

"If pictures of us on this bridge get out of the world, the police will arrive and arrest us."

"Oh." Lily giggled and allowed him the kiss. "Yes, I would rather an engagement ring over a pair of police bracelets."

"Oh, you would?" Ned raised his eyebrows as they began walking hand-in-hand across the bridge to their waiting car.

"Yes, would you?"

Ned nodded. "Yes, not getting arrested would be the best way to go."

Lily stopped. "And the engagement ring?"

"I don't need one of those."

"Oh, well never mind then," Lily shrugged and moved a step ahead.

"Let's go buy some pizza. My treat," Ned said as he opened her car door for her.

Lily ducked inside. "That'll be – owee!"

"What's wrong?" Ned dropped to a knee to help her.

"I sat on some—" Lily had drawn a small velvet box from beneath her. She looked from it to Ned with a joyous grin.

"See, I don't need engagement rings. I already have some." Ned smiled and kissed her. "Will you wear yours?"

"Forever and always," Lily opened the box and allowed him to take and place the white gold ring on her finger. He had a similar one for himself as well.

"Thank you, sweetheart. A slice of pepperoni pizza will be heaven-lily, now." Ned beamed as he climbed behind the wheel and headed off with her into the rest of their lives together.

Callisto's Celestial Plan

Dusk had fallen on the Marin household. The youngest member of the family was curled in the bay window of her bedroom. She was watching the stars emerge one by one in the ever-darkening velveteen sky. Even if just twelve-years-old, she loved the stars, the planets – she dreamed of being an astronaut one day. Her mother Juliet must have known she'd be a cosmic girl having named her Callisto. The little girl knew Callisto was the third-largest moon in the solar system and the second-largest of the Jovian moons of Jupiter. The knowledge made her proud of her name.

"There's Polaris the North Star so the Big Dipper or Plough constellation is going to appear there tonight." Callisto mused to herself, as she spun her globe star chart and found the Ursa Major constellation. With a smile, she refocused on the now indigo to midnight-blue sky, imagining piloting a starship visiting the planets.

It was then the front door slammed and something smashed close to the bottom of the stairs. The ruckus was followed by a fleshy thud and a feminine groan of pain.

Callisto squeezed her eyes shut as tears fell on her cheeks. She knew her daddy Leroy had returned from work and he was drunk. She wished it was an aberration, an unusual event but it wasn't. Most nights he'd come home in a blind rage, he'd break things and worse he'd hurt her mother.

"Where's mah dinner, yer worthless wench!" he slurred at the top of his lungs as something else was thundered into the wall with a tinkle of glass.

Callisto's mother whimpered in pain. "It's coming, please stop hurting me!"

Callisto unfurled herself from the bay window and took off her dressing gown. She'd allowed her mum to think, she'd showered and undressed for the night. But Callisto wasn't sleeping here tonight, she couldn't bear her daddy's violence any more. Standing in her favourite, warm blue dress and loafers, she was determined to change things for the better. "I'll show you, daddy," she said whilst wiping her eyes and leaving her room with a cloth bag in hand. Looking back at the star globe, she let out a saddened sniff. It was a shame to leave it but it wouldn't fit in the bag. Heading downstairs, she unlocked and opened the front door and turned off the light switch. Leaving her bag on the doorstep, she flinched as the shouting returned.

"I've been working mah arse off all day, woman. Look at yer, ya done nothin' – sod all. No cleanin' done, no laundry, mah dinner isn't even ready. You're a worthless disgusting mess!"

Callisto clenched her fists, infuriated by her daddy's words. She marched into the lounge and gasped. The room had been clean before; she knew her mummy had been doing housework all day. Now, he'd come home and wrecked everything as usual. A whole basket of freshly washed and ironed clothes were strewn about the floor. A dog ornament was smashed in the fireplace. Callisto let out a sob as her foot scrunched a piece of crumpled paper. She'd painted a lovely picture of the house with stars and planets above it this afternoon. Her daddy had torn it to bits and chucked it around the room.

"I did all the housework you ungrateful, git! You're drunk! You ruined everything! I'll do—" Juliet screamed. Her voice trailed off with a gurgle.

When Callisto dared to enter the kitchen, she saw her daddy holding her mum by the throat. His veins and muscles were bulging with anger around his blue work trousers and shirt. His eyes were bloodshot and his blond hair a mess. It terrified her, but she had to provoke him. "I hate you, Daddy. I'll make sure you don't hurt Mummy a—"

Leroy hurled Juliet into the sink unit causing her to cry out in pain. He rounded on his daughter and cracked her across the face with the back of his hand. She fell back into the lounge. He cursed and stalked after her. "I'm yer daddy, Callie. You'll do as I say!" he grunted, his alcohol breath fouling the room.

Callisto glared at him as she backpedalled across the room with a bruise forming on her cheek and blood oozing from a nostril. "You're not my daddy. Daddies are nice and you're a nasty, rotten drunk!"

"I will make you take that back, you little witch." Leroy lunged for his daughter.

She was ready for him. The little girl slammed her trainer deep into his groin with a satisfying thud.

Pain and his drunken stupor caused him to stagger around and fall over the coffee table.

Callisto leapt to her feet, grabbed her bag and fled the house. She smirked at the sight of her daddy falling over the table – it was good revenge. The mirth faded fast though. She knew she could never return home so long as he lived here now. Running beneath the starry sky as fast as possible, she focused on her plan. Time to hide and wait for daddy to catch himself.

The little girl enjoyed her small town by the sea. Light pollution was low allowing her to see billions of stars stretching away to the horizon over the North Sea. She slowed to a walk and wandered along a sandy path amid the marram grasses and dunes. The whole way her eyes remained glued to the starscape. She picked out the constellations Orion, Ophiuchus, Hercules, Ursa Minor and Major among others. Close to the horizon, she could see the red glow of a familiar planet.

"One day I'll find a way to reach you, Mars. First I have to you make sure my daddy doesn't kill me or Mummy."

Callisto wiped her eyes as she scanned the sky. She began to imagine the planets aligned in the sky above her. In her mind, she could use moonbeams as shining ropes to lasso the planets. They become the most magical of balloons to carry her to a far-off and safe world.

Lost in her galactic thoughts, Callisto's feet carried her on to the beach. She headed away from town and kept going until the sand became rocky and the dunes gave way to cliffs. She'd found ammonite and belemnite fossils in the rock pools here in the not-too-distant past. Daddy used to be nice then. He'd take her out for days, they'd share ice cream and go on fairground rides. He'd even take her to the zoo in the next town. She knew that daddy was long gone. The demons in the alcohol had ensured he'd never come back. Callisto couldn't help it – those thoughts left her crying as she hugged herself and walked on.

The blue flickering lights of a police car raced along the seafront. Judging by the direction they took, Callisto felt they might be going to her home. She climbed over some rocks and tucked herself into a cave within the cliff. It wasn't a particularly deep cave but it gave a little roof and shelter. Callisto had wandered in here on nights before and proclaimed it the North Star Cave. It was the perfect name; Polaris sat in the sky right in the middle of the opening as she looked out. Discovering this cave had given her the courage to put her plan of action.

Callisto had learned lots from her daddy when he was nice. She collected a little driftwood and using his flint and striker soon had a little fire started. Taking a deep breath, she began to relax within the crackling warmth of the glowing flames. Reaching into her bag, she took out a large bar of chocolate. "Daddy will be furious when he realises, I've eaten you." The little girl chuckled as she tore off the brown wrapper and put the first chunk in her mouth.

Allowing it to melt slowly, she savoured the rich, creamy, slightly bitter notes of chocolate. Using her bag as a pillow, she lay down and continued to enjoy the confection whilst watching the fire.

The first her thoughts were of home. Was her mummy okay? What else had her daddy done? What would he do to her if he caught her? Soon tiredness crept in as the flickering flames lulled him to sleep. As if by magic she was floating beneath her planetary balloons. She giggled as she flew over Orion's belt, splashed her feet in the waters of Neptune and passed through the rings of Saturn. Then she was on the surface of Mars. Martians did live here. They weren't green or grey, but quite regular as humans go. They called themselves the Anunnaki as they proudly showed her around. They revealed Mars used to be like Earth until it moved away from the sun. Callisto had just entered a crater home belonging to an Anunnaki family when everything began to shake.

"Callie! Callie? Are you alright?" said a voice as somebody shook her shoulder. "I'm a police lady called, Lucy."

"Lucy?" Callisto returned to Earth and opened her eyes with a groan. That had been such a good dream. "My face hurts but I'm okay, thank you," she replied as she took in the uniform of a friendly, smiling policewoman with a bun of blonde hair. Beyond her was a male police constable looking pleased to see her.

"That's a relief! It's good to see you, Callie." the policewoman spoke into her radio. "Officer Lucy Green to dispatch. We have Callie safe and sound."

"It's Callisto. I'm named after Jupiter's second moon," said the little girl standing up.

"Oh really? Why not the first moon then?" asked Lucy looking interested.

Callisto giggled. "Because Ganymede makes a terrible name."

"No kidding! That sounds horrible." Lucy chuckled, put an arm around her and helped her from the cave.

"Please don't take me home. Daddy will kill me. He was going to kill Mummy tonight." Callisto felt her fears return as the policeman shone his torch toward her. He gently touched the bruising on her face causing her to flinch in pain.

"Did your Daddy do this?" he asked.

Callisto nodded and moved her face away from his hand. She couldn't stop her tears flowing down her face, knowing she had to face her dad soon.

"Hey, don't worry it's going to be okay now. Your mummy will be okay. Your daddy has been arrested for assaulting her. He is going to be arrested for hitting you too. The judge will punish and ensure he cannot come near or do anything to either of you again."

"Really? That'll be great."

"Really," said Lucy giving her a grin. Let's go and see the paramedic and make sure you're okay. Then get you back to your mummy, okay?"

"Thank you." Callisto smiled. Her plan had worked. She knew if she ran away and disappeared long enough the police would have to get involved. If they did so they'd learn what her daddy did and punish him for it. Now that was happening, Callisto knew, she and her mummy could enjoy life and stargaze together in happiness.

Cassidy's Song

"Just think, in two days this park will be buzzing with people all here to listen to you perform," Brady said with a glance at the traditional, hexagonal park bandstand. Beneath the trees on the wide lawns, it was a natural stage for beautiful music.

"I can't do it." Cassidy took a deep shaky breath and turned away from him. She gathered her curls of auburn hair over her right shoulder and began to walk away.

"Why? I'm so excited to watch you perform. I want to feel the pride as everybody cheers for the musical princess I love." Brady stopped her leaving by interlinking his fingers in hers and gently turning her to face him.

"I'm scared, Brady. I've never performed in front of anyone like that before."

"That's a natural feeling. You're such a wonderful performer your musical soul is indigenous to that stage. I know once you begin you'll relax and love every second of your performance."

Cassidy shook her head. "I'm sorry, I won't be coming."

Brady looked from her fearful eyes to the trees surrounding the park. He knew how she was feeling but felt strongly that she could do it. Somehow, he had to help her find a way to conquer those nerves. "Wait here, okay?"

Cassidy nodded.

"Thank you." Brady graced her lips with a kiss and jogged away to the sheltered housing estate for the elderly bordering the park. Cassidy's grandmother lived there. She had something Brady required.

Within ten minutes, he was jogging back toward Cassidy. She'd taken to sitting on the lawn. Wearing her little khaki shorts and lacy camo-vest, she looked a little like a scared elf.

"Brady, why do you have my guitar?" she asked.

"I asked your grandmother to let me borrow it." He held out a hand. "Come on."

"No, what are you doing?"

"I'm asking you to trust me," Brady smiled. "Please."

"Okay," Cassidy sighed and accepted his hand to regain her feet.

Brady led her to the red-brick and green railed bandstand. He could feel her shrinking away as they ascended the steps. "It's okay," he told her with a cheery wink.

"What are you doing?" Cassidy said as she scanned the park for people as if they were lions and she was a vulnerable baby gazelle.

"I'm making sure you don't lose what is a magical opportunity," Brady held out her guitar. "This is yours. Play a little something for me."

Cassidy took her acoustic guitar and slipped the strap over her head. "Please don't make me do this."

"I have to. You're too special to be caged by fear. You have to do this and let the people hear your beautiful voice and music," Brady took a deep breath and nodded.

Two sparkling tears dropped onto Cassidy's cheeks and flowed off her chin.

"Hey, don't cry, it's okay." Brady stepped right in front of her. "Do you see my eyes?"

Cassidy nodded.

"Good, what colour are they?"

"Brown."

"Yes. Can you feel the energy coming from them?" Brady smiled as he felt her eyes connecting with his.

"I feel like you adore me and that I'll let you down if I don't do this." Cassidy broke the gaze and looked at the guitar in her arms.

"I love everything about you and you'll never disappoint me. Now, look at me. Look at my ugly face and feel my love hugging you and…"

Cassidy giggled. "You're so silly, and not a bit ugly."

"Thank you," Brady grinned. He'd hoped the description would at least draw a smile. "Now, as you feel my love holding your hands, allow the bandstand to melt away as you begin to play for me."

Cassidy took a breath and focused on his eyes as her fingers began to strum the strings of her guitar.

Brady began to nod to the rhythm. He could feel her nerves and the hummingbird-like thrum of her heart but he urged her on with a confident nod. "Yes, my wonderful, Cassidy. You can do this!"

Cassidy allowed her fingers to change the notes and then she began to sing with a shiver of nervousness edging her soulful voice.

♫ *Flowers in the fields*
That's you and I
We shine with love that never yields
We'll never fade and never die. ♫

Brady beamed. Her beautiful song washed over him like that of a sirens call. How he longed to hold and kiss her as he watched on full of desire and adoration. He applauded as Cassidy finished her song.

Someone else joined in from beyond the bandstand. "That was beautiful! I hope you're performing that on Saturday night," he called.

"I'm n—" Cassidy began.

"She'll be here," Brady said as he held her trembling hands.

"Awesome, see you Saturday." The man waved and walked away with his dog.

"Brady, please. I still won't be able to perform in a park full of people on Saturday. I have to be on stage alone and I can't do that. Please, don't make me do this." Cassidy freed herself and walked towards the steps.

"If you promise to walk on to the stage on Saturday, I promise you will never be alone." Brady led her down from the bandstand. "Will you promise?"

Cassidy nodded. "I promise to try."

"That's all I ask," Brady hugged her. "At least I don't have to drag you on stage by your cute little toes now."

"Huh, that would earn you a slap!" Cassidy giggled as they walked from the park hand in hand.

Saturday night came warm and sultry beneath the starry sky. The bank holiday music festival was attended by at least five thousand people. Both the bandstand and the park railings had been adorned by swathes of glittering lights.

"This is it, ten minutes and one beautiful song and you'll be home free," Brady whispered in Cassidy's ear as he danced with her to the beat of a rock 'n' roll band's song.

"That's if I don't die of fright first!" Cassidy replied as the song ended.

"Course you won't! You'll do yourself proud up there," said her grandmother giving her shoulder a confident squeeze.

"Thank you, Nan." Cassidy gave a nervous smile.

"You do need to stop trembling though; you're shaking me to bits." Brady grinned and poked her nose fondly to elicit a giggle.

"Hey! I do appreciate you doing this for me. I just hope I can—"

"Ladies and gentlemen give it up for the Slated Eighties!"

said the evening's compere. The gentleman was dressed in a bright red suit and doing a grand job of keeping the audience loud and happy.

The audience applauded, cheered, and whistled as the band bowed and left the bandstand.

"Up next, we have a new and young singing sensation. A talented singer and guitarist from right here in our wonderful city. Please give it up for Cassidy Newman!"

"Go and enchant them, sweetheart!" Brady kissed her as he led the way to the steps holding her hand.

She looked back as her fingers slipped from his. Fear gripped her as she faced the climb to the stage alone. "You promised!" she said through teary eyes as the crowds cheered for her.

"I did," Brady winked. "I love you, go on!"

Cassidy smoothed her indigo evening dress and gulped as she reached the stage. Picking up her guitar, she approached the microphone. "I er – good evening, everyone!"

"Ready?" whispered the DJ preparing to start her soundtrack.

Cassidy could hear her teeth chattering through her skull. She'd come over so hot she was sure she'd collapse. Taking a sip of water from a bottle she'd left with her guitar, she nodded. "Okay." With her feet screaming for her to run she tried to compose herself.

Turning to face her audience, she gasped. They'd all switched on their phone lights creating the feeling of being on the biggest stage. One light was closer than the others.

Brady was sitting cross-legged on the bandstand with his back against the railings. "Feel my love holding your hands, allow the bandstand to melt away and sing," he urged.

Cassidy beamed through teary eyes. She took a deep breath and nodded to him as she began to play with the music.

♫ *Flowers in the fields*
That's you and I
We shine with love that never yields
We'll never fade and never die. ♫

The audience gave a collective gasp as Cassidy made it through the first chorus. As one they began waving their lights creating a truly romantic scene.

♫ *Know I'm here for you*
Whatever darkness grows
Together we'll see it through
Love stronger than a blooming rose. ♫

Brady punched the air in delight. "You got this, beautiful!"

♫ *Flowers in the fields*
That's you and I
We shine with love that never yields
We'll never fade and never die. ♫

Cassidy felt her nerves melting away as she sang with all her heart,

♫ *Two hearts spliced together*
Petals shining through the gloom
Our love growing forever
In a field of eternal bloom ♫

Cassidy was one chorus away now. As she began the opening line the audience began to sing it with her.

♫ *Flowers in the fields*
That's you and I
We shine with love that never yields
We'll never fade and never die ♫

Cassidy sang the last word and dropped the stage into

an eerie silence. For a moment she felt as if the audience were shocked by how bad she'd been. Then they erupted with cheers and applause.

"Yeah!" Brady yelled with the audience. He bounded to his feet and threw his arms around her. "You were incredible!"

"That was amazing! Thank you so much, Brady." Cassidy kissed him before taking a bow before her new fans. "Did you get them to put their lights on?"

"Amazing what a request in the show programme can do, isn't it?" Brady said.

"You're amazing; that was so special," Cassidy said holding him with all her heart.

"Ladies and gentlemen, the amazing Cassidy Newman!" announced the compere returning to the bandstand.

Cassidy took another bow. "Thank you, have a good evening, everyone!" she said into the microphone with a wave.

Brady led her down the steps. "Whatever darkness grows, together we'll see it through."

"Yes, I think we will!" Cassidy agreed.

"So, can you sing on stage in front of a large audience now?"

"As long as you're with me, I know I can," Cassidy replied with a smile at her proud grandmother. She knew then Brady had given her a start at a wonderful musical life.

Cupid's Blessing

The girl with the luscious, auburn hair and heart-warming smile in the photograph is Taylor Laine. Sean loved her so much. He wiped his eyes and forced himself to look away from her picture. Saturday, he'd made a terrible mistake. It happened whilst clubbing with Taylor. She'd gone to fresh up in the Ladies. Sean took the chance to get more drinks. At the bar, a curvaceous blonde had approached and kissed him. Taylor had seen the uninvited smooch and fled. Now, she wouldn't even answer a text or call from him.

Sean couldn't stand the pain of hurting the one he loved. "I'm so, sorry for hurting you," he told her picture with tears moistening his cheeks. Moving to collapse on his bed, he watched a seashell tumble from the chest of drawers to the floor. He jolted into a sitting position. Nothing had touched the shell and nobody was in the room to cause it to fall. There was something though, a picture of his grandfather on the wall. Was he dropping the shell as a message to go for a walk?

Sean felt compelled to go for a walk then. He pulled on his trainers and fled the house to clear his head. Living in the crabbing town of Cromer was ideal for that. He ran to the clifftop and down the winding slope to the beach promenade. It ran for over a mile either side of the pier. The beach here was very stony to protect the eroding clay cliffs. It did have wonderfully sandy areas and rock pools between some revetments too.

Sean jogged toward the pier avoiding inquisitive dogs, children having fun and a few couples enjoying the late afternoon. The sun would soon touch the horizon with its golden fingers creating a beautiful late afternoon.

Someway ahead of him, a female wearing a cream dress caught his attention. She took a phone from her pink-hoodie pocket. In doing so, something fell and skittered off the promenade and fell onto the beach. She never seemed to notice as she carried on toward the pier.

Sean leapt the four feet down onto the beach and jogged over the stones and sand. There was the object between a large flint and smaller pebbles, a pretty mother-of-pearl compact mirror and make-up case.

Scooping it up, Sean made for the next steps and regained the promenade. He was forced to duck through a cloud of seagulls attempting to mug a gentleman of his fish and chips. Grinning, he scanned the path for the lady. She was a good way ahead and passing the pier, and so he set off to catch her.

The pier boasted a cafe, gift shop, theatre, and the lifeboat station on the seaward end. None of those interested the lady. She walked right on by and followed the slope to the next section of the beach.

Sean followed and caught her just as she arrived at the sand. "Excuse me, madam. You dropped your compact back there."

The lady removed her hood revealing glossy auburn hair. Turning to greet him, her soft face turned harsh with bitterness. "You! Get away from me!"

"Taylor!" Tears stung Sean's eyes as he saw the anguish etched on her face. "Oh, Taylor. I'm so sorry. Please let me talk to you. I never meant for any of this to happen."

The breeze blew her hair about her face as she hugged herself. "Why should I? You kissed that blonde bimbo right in front of me."

"No. No, Taylor. I was at the bar ordering drinks. She came onto and kissed me without my permission. I never asked for it, I never wanted it. I—"

"How can I trust you again!" Taylor wiped her eyes and made to walk away.

"Please give me a chance!"

"No – go away!" Taylor stomped her foot, burst into tears and started running.

Sean caught her and turned her to face him. "Wait. Let me talk to you."

"I don't want to hear it. If you can kiss a vivacious woman like her. There's no hope for you loving plain old me," she cried behind her hands.

"Look, I don't claim to be the most virtuous, ethical man on the planet." Sean took her shaking hands. "On my honour, I love you just as you are. You have the most beautiful mind, body and soul. All she had was big breasts and the attitude of a hideous succubus. I could never love her."

"Easy for you to say that after what you did with her!" Taylor freed herself stalked off again.

"Please. Don't go!" Sean found himself under the disapproving gaze of two elderly ladies. He glared at them before trudging after the one he loved. "Taylor, look. Take my phone and check the contacts and social media. You know how to search for new numbers and connections."

Taylor reached the wooden revetment covered in seaweed and barnacles before she came to a stop. "What would that prove, huh?" She demanded to know but took her compact back and the phone all the same.

Sean watched her unlock and begin checking the phone. He hid a smile; she was giving him a chance. "If the kiss-stealer meant anything to me, she'd be in there, right? She's not there, she never will be. If you'd have looked back in the nightclub; you would have seen me push her off and come to apologise to you." Sean bit back tears. "But you ran away from me – you never gave me a chance."

Silence fell to Taylor flicking about on the phone.

All he could do was watch her. He could tell by the

reflections in her pretty hazel eyes, she was checking his Facebook and Twitter among other places.

"You don't love her?" She said at last with a shudder of emotion. The setting sun worked its magic, turning her tears golden upon her cheeks.

Sean shook his head. "Never. I'm so, so sorry you saw her kiss me. She meant nothing to me and never will." Sean dropped to a knee before her and held out a hand. He had to do all he could to reconcile with her. He was lost so long as Taylor wasn't by his side. "My love and my heart belong to you."

Taylor removed her hoodie revealing the pretty lace bodice of her dress. She hung the garment on the revetment and placed her sandals beneath. Ignoring Sean's hand, she walked down to the shore and allowed the gentle waves to curl over her toes.

Sean sighed and shook his head as he watched her. His heart was close to breaking at the realisation he may never be reconciled with her. Standing again, he removed his trainers and followed her. "Look, if you need more proof, we can even examine the CCTV at the nightclub. I'm sure they won't mind."

She shook her head. "I saw the messages you left me and the missed calls. I'm sorry, I didn't answer you."

"No, don't be. After what you saw, why would you?" He gave her a small smile. "You know, this is the first time I left my room since that happened. Without your love, encouragement and beautiful smile I have nothing worth living for."

Taylor blushed, she dipped her foot in the salty water and flicked it at him. Her aim was good, and she managed to soak his shirt and trousers.

"Hey, Cheeky!" Sean chuckled and made to splash her back. He adored the squeal and smile she gave him. He didn't carry through with the threat. Instead, stopping and adoring her. "This is what I imagine my life with you to be like. Romantic frivolity every day. I love you, Taylor."

As the sky turned a sublime orange, she approached and took his hand. "Today was the first day I left my home too. I don't know why but something told me I should go for a walk. When I took my phone out and lost my compact, I had a Facebook message. I thought it was from you." Gazing into his eyes, she seemed to take a minute to contemplate the situation. "It was a spam thing from a dating site. Weirdly, the message was completely blank."

"Makes perfect sense to me." Sean took a deep breath, bringing her close and absorbing her energy. Feeling her living and breathing against him, left him alive and euphoric. "Cupid brought us together. He made us both come out for a walk. He allowed me a chance to apologise by giving me your compact. I want to thank you for letting me talk with you. I also understand if you don't trust and can't be with me any—"

"Thank you, Sean." Taylor dropped her hand on his shoulder and brushed her nose against his as they kissed. They stood together silhouetted in the sun for a long moment. Neither saw it vanish over the horizon or felt its last rays. Even the rising water failed to register with them. They were lost in each other and love once more.

Despondent, Worthless and Hidden

It had been a slow steady decline over the last few months. Evan had tried to help but Vicky but she was so dependent, she wouldn't let him in. Day after day, Vicky's mood continued to drop into melancholy. Her low-spirits cast hopelessness into the ether of the house to a point Evan was becoming oppressed as well. Yet try as he might, she wouldn't let him help. Despite that, he knew a breakpoint was coming.

Requiring a drink, Evan entered the kitchen on Tuesday afternoon. Vicky was there wearing a pretty blue summer dress and looking withdrawn through lack of sleep. She was cooking dinner as she loved to do.

Evan poured two glasses of orange juice. "Here you—"

Vicky cracked an egg and poured most of it on the work surface.

Evan's heart broke like the egg as she burst into tears, clasped her shaking hands to her head and lowered herself against the counter sobbing as if her world had shattered. "Hey, come on, Vicky. It's only an egg. Will you tell me what's wrong?"

Vicky's tears continued to fall like the egg dripping onto the floor but she said nothing.

Evan placed a hand on her trembling shoulder. "You've been getting so despondent for a while now. Please let me help you."

Vicky shrugged him off, dried her eyes and pulled some kitchen paper from the roll.

Evan took it from her and threw it on the counter. "Forget the egg, I'm worried about you."

"I'll be fine. Let me finish dinner."

"I can't do that. You used to be the brightest ray of sunshine in my life. Now, you've been shrouded in darkness

41

for weeks. I love you with all my heart and I want to see your sparkle again."

"I'm sorry, Evee, I know I'm failing you too?" Vicky's face creased into anguish as she sobbed again. "I – I hate leaving you to earn all the money and pay all the bills but I'm useless. I'm completely worthless."

"Hey, that's not true. You'll never fail me; it's just taking time for you to get a job, that's all." Evan wrapped her in his arms. "You're worth the world to me, you know that."

"You should get a new partner. One who's able to work and help you with bills instead of being a helpless wretch."

"I never realised you felt that way about yourself and what you do around here. I wish you'd have told me."

Vicky couldn't help sobbing against his shoulder. "It's so unfair. I've got the best qualifications; and I've gained all the experience I need. And they still made me redundant. It's been nearly six months ago. All those hundreds of places I've applied to. Nobody wants me. I'm useless."

"No you're not. It's not you at all. The economy is shot to hell and businesses are closing everywhere. Over a thousand people are going for every available job. Those businesses you applied to, likely never even knew they had a star among the stack of shadows on their desk. They—"

"Shouldn't matter, Evan. My CV should be good enough but something about me makes me unemployable. It must do; I can't even get a bloody interview!" Vicky freed herself and dropped onto a dining chair – a picture of despair and hopelessness.

Evan knelt down in front of her. "Listen – my boss advertises for employees from time to time. He gets a huge stack of applications and resumés on his desk and he never reads most of them."

"What, that's a lie! Why would he do that?"

42

"Simple. He hasn't got the time or the need to read them all. He simply selects a random ten resumés, interviews the best of those, employs someone, and dumps the rest in the shredder. I guarantee that's happening to you too. You're a special, talented lady who'd get the job in a heartbeat if they read your application."

"You really think that's why I can't get work?" Vicky looked at him for the first time, tears twinkling in her eyes.

Evan nodded and smiled at her as he took the kitchen paper and dried her eyes. He followed it with a kiss as he smoothed her hair behind an ear. "No, I know so and I'm going to prove it tomorrow," he said with determination.

"How?"

"I'm taking the day off and we're going job hunting in a different way. A way that'll show the employers how shiny and perfect for the job you are."

"I don't know; I'll probably disappoint you." Vicky locked eyes with him looking nervous.

"Not possible and this will work. It has to because I want my beautiful, courageous ray of sunshine back." Evan cleaned the kitchen and finished dinner. After eating he sat with Vicky and went over her C.V. They made a couple of adjustments and printed a stack.

The next day he put Vicky in the car and the two drove to a list of businesses requiring a senior nutritionist with bachelors and masters degrees. Each time, Evan gave her a little pep-talk and sent her inside looking professional and confident in her smart midnight-blue skirt suit. Her goal; to ask to speak with the manager hiring for the role. She would then introduce herself and what she could do for the company as she handed over her CV. Each time she did that she proved she really wanted the job and was perfect for it.

By the end of the day, Vicky was tired but standing a

little straighter. She was looking more confident and her despondence was pushed to the back of her mind.

By the end of the week, Vicky had four interviews. Evan proudly took her to each one and helped her in every way he could. For him to see her working and happy was a labour of love. He didn't care about the money but if she wanted to work and earn, he would see it so and make her smile again.

The first Monday of the next month, Vicky was all smiles as she began her new job as the smart, confident, happy lady Evan had fallen in love with several years ago.

Remember this. An emailed or posted C.V is unlikely to be read due to the high volume the employers receive. Dress in your nicest suit and hand-deliver it to the employer. Show them you are the person they need to hire and your chances of success will be so much higher. Good Luck.

Ecstasy of Spirit

It wasn't Kari's fault she needed the high. Some unknown person had put the ecstasy in her drink when she turned fourteen. That trip had been amazing; she loved the way the MDMA made her vision sharper, the colours more vivid. How it took the music at the party to a mesmerising almost hypnotic place. The ecstasy took away all her anxieties, social and life issues and made everything feel fine. It ramped her senses up to the max and life was great. Sure she'd been sick after but all she wanted was more.

Now, Kari was seventeen, she'd just survived school with barely passable grades. Every weekend she was dosing up on ecstasy and she was nothing like the smart and pretty girl she used to be. She looked so tired, gaunt and skinny. Even as she pulled her dry blonde hair into a ponytail, she saw herself in the mirror and grimaced. She knew the damage she was doing to herself – she could see it. It didn't matter at all; she'd had no ecstasy since Saturday and was growing desperate. The Tuesday blues were in full effect and she had to get another fix fast.

Kari pulled on her trainers and left her untidy bedroom.

"Where are you going, Kari?" asked a stern voice.

"Out." Kari glared at her father, John. A farmer of forty years.

"No, you're not," he said, barring the way.

"I'm seventeen. You can't stop me!" Kari yelled. She slipped under his arm and dashed down the stairs. At the bottom, she wrenched open the front door and ran into the cottage garden.

"I won't let you get another fix. I can't bear to see you like this anymore." John ran around his daughter and stopped her at the gate. "I failed you by letting you get in this far. I won't let you go any further."

She saw he was on the verge of crying. "It's not your fault. Now, let me go!" Kari ran across the garden and leapt the drystone wall.

John was through the gate and holding her arm in a heartbeat. "I said no! Now, please, get back inside."

Kari lost control. "No, let me go you're hurting me!" she screamed and wrenched, kicked and flailed at him but he wouldn't let her go.

"Stop, please! I don't want to hurt you, sweetheart." John begged with tears streaming down his face.

Kari landed a withering slap and bounded free.

John caught her shoulder and turned her around, she tripped and fell. "I'm sorry. I won't let you go this time."

"Let her go, John. This isn't the way," said a new deeper voice.

Kari forced herself on to a side and saw her father's chief shepherd, Herod, standing there. She'd known him all her life. This was the first time she'd seen him looking so mournful.

"Herod, I can't let her get more drugs."

"I understand, John. We've been friends for many years now. Will you trust me with your daughter?"

"Of course. What will you do?"

"He'll do nothing to me!" Kari screamed and tried again to break free.

"Kari, I am your friend, Herod. Remember all the times you came to play with the lambs. I beg you, remember how I taught you to mother and feed the babies. Do you remember how I cared for you when you were sick those times when your mother and father couldn't be here?" Herod said.

Kari nodded and wiped away tears.

"Good." Herod looked toward John and received a nod. He gave Kari a smile and held out a hand. "Come with me."

"No, I have to go to, Ben. Both of you leave me alone!" Kari kicked out at her dad and bounded to her feet. She made to run but she couldn't go, Herod's voice held her in place. She turned to face him, taking in his waxed trench coat, fleece jumper and trousers. More than that she took in his craggy face and wise blue eyes. The braids in his wiry white hair. It was like she was seeing him for the first time.

"Ben will only give you demons, Deerheart. I will give you something far more powerful. You want the pain and suffering to go away. You walk away from the drugs and follow me." Herod winked at her and turned to walk away. "Go and have some tea, John. Kari will be safe with me."

Kari gave her dad a sorrowful look and despite herself followed Herod. He led her over the fields of grazing sheep and cows. She thought he was going to his little stone hut on the hill. Instead, he cut a path into the woods.

"I'm glad you decided to follow me, Kari. I've watched you succumb to the demons for too long. You were once a special girl; it's not too late to be her again." Herod pulled back a birch branch and beckoned Kari into a clearing.

Kari perched on a rock. She watched him gathering sticks and making preparations for a fire. She couldn't help sadness welling within her and tears flowing down her face. "Why won't people just let me have what I need to be happy? I don't fit in. Classes make me anxious and people scare me. The ecstasy makes all that go away."

"I understand, dear heart." Herod scraped his knife along a piece of flint casting sparks into his tinder. Within moments he was kindling a crackling, warm fire. "Much better. Join me at the fire."

Kari saw the kind old man smiling at her and sat by him at the fireside. The warmth radiated through her almost hugging her. "What will you do to me? To make me better, I mean."

"What would you have me do? Beat some discipline into you. Exorcize you, perhaps?"

47

"Is that what I need?"

Herod laughed. "No, you just need to find yourself and your hidden strength is all."

"How? I'm weak and useless." Kari felt her shoulder tremble as sadness poured from her.

"Not at all. You were a brave special young lady before the drugs. You shall be again. Now, Trust me." Herod took a deep breath, rose and stood behind her. "Close your eyes and take a deep breath… That's it, find a nice deep rhythm."

Kari did, she felt him kneel behind her as she sucked in and breathed out. His strangely warm hands touched her temples softly.

"Focus now."

Kari allowed herself to relax and concentrated on her breathing.

"Good. You're safe, Deerheart. Find the white light. With every breath in you take, I want you to make that light, and with it your spirit, bigger. Make them stronger!"

Kari focused and there was the light. Herod's fingers rotated on her temples creating a tingling through her body. She willed the light to be bigger, the tingling grew strong.

"I feel it. Now on every exhale cast out those things which give the demon strength. You are as brave as the deer and stronger than the mighty oxen."

"I am," Kari whispered.

Kari heard him howl like a wolf. His hands smoothed over her ponytail and she could feel him no more.

"How do you feel?" Herod asked.

"My body's tingling. I feel light, buzzing, energetic. I'm…" Kari couldn't describe the wonderful feeling pulsing through her body.

"Ecstatic? Euphoric maybe?" Herod offered.

"Yes. I—" Something brushed her hands.

"Relax, it's okay."

Kari felt a nuzzling near her chest, her cheek. "What's here?"

"Open your eyes and remain calm," Herod instructed.

Kari did; the fire was gone. It was dusky in the woods and there before her was a beautiful specked fallow deer doe. Kari smiled and put out her fingers.

The deer pushed her face against her hands.

"How?" Kari tickled the deer's chin and beamed the ecstasy of the moment strong within her.

"Only those pure of heart can call upon the creatures. I awakened your spirit to cast out the demon in your body. With it gone your soul cast out for help and this beautiful deer answered."

Kari reached forward and kissed the doe on the nose.

It nuzzled her for a moment longer and cantered into the woods.

Kari rose and approached Herod. He'd sat away from her on a fallen log at the edge of the clearing. She put her arms around him and hugged tight. "Thank you for sharing your magic with me."

"I cast no spells. It was all you." Herod took a small deer doe, carved from oak, out of his trench coat pocket. It was on a simple black thread. "My grandfather carved me this. He told me whenever I needed help the animals would always be here for me. He was never wrong." Herod carefully placed the doe around Kari's neck and smiled at her. "It's time you carried her, Deerheart."

"I—" Kari took the doe in her shaking hands. It felt light and yet energised with magic somehow. "Thank you."

"There's no need for that. Just promise me, whenever the demon calls to you. Come out here, kindle a small fire and summon your spirit light and allow the animals to carry away your demons. Will you do that?" Herod asked.

Kari hugged him again. "I will. Thank you so much."

"Then, home you go."

Kari smiled and set off with a newfound ecstasy for life in her soul. She ran all the way home and burst inside. She found her dad in their old kitchen and hugged him for all she was worth, apologising for all the trouble she caused. He burst into tears at seeing his daughter's eyes sparkling with life for the first time in three years.

Over the coming days, Kari rid herself of the drugs and began to excel at college. She would call upon her spirit and the doe a lot to get through it, but she would make it now; Herod had seen it so. Though Kari tried to find Herod to thank him, the old shepherd had vanished never to be seen again.

Ride to the Rescue

There's nothing better than a warm fire crackling in the grate on a cold winter's day. Even twelve-year-old Millie Oates had to admit that. It was Saturday so she didn't have to be at school. Millie was considered lucky by her friends. She lived on a farm with her parents. Even now her dad was out dealing with the sheep. She could hear mother baking in the kitchen too; there was always something delicious to eat around the farmhouse.

Millie had already been out feeding her Connemara ponies this morning. Now, she sat on the rug before the fire, sketching in her book. She loved to draw and was top of her art class.

It was always a mystery to Millie why her father listened to the police radio. Even now, she could hear police officers calling in incidents through the device on the dining table. Millie felt listening to police business was a little sneaky – even shady.

"Suspect car has turned left, left, left onto Coney Lane. That's left onto Coney Lane. I can confirm kidnapped girl is in the back."

"He's coming this way!" Millie bounded to her feet, sending her sketchbook and pencils flying across the hearth. She quickly crossed the flagstone floor into the hall. The walls were all cedar panelled here. The intrepid girl pulled her riding boots on over her jeans, tied back her chestnut hair, and raced out the front door.

Following the gravel drive around the ivy-covered farmhouse, she arrived at her stables. There were twelve stalls in all, each home to a Connemara pony. Millie ignored those and clambered over the fence into the paddock. Even before her feet landed in the grass, she let out a whistle. "Let's go, Candesco!"

51

This speckled grey pony nickered and nodded his head as he cantered around behind his favourite human.

Millie ran alongside him, jumped on a hay bale and vaulted onto the ponies back. She had no saddle, just reins, but that didn't worry her. Millie had been riding all her life and was confident bareback. "Ya! Come on, Candesco – Somebody needs our help!" Millie directed him across the paddock. Without blinking an eye, she gave a pull on the reins. Pony and girl leapt the fence and set off at a gallop.

It was as though, Candesco and Millie were connected at the soul when riding together. He seemed to anticipate her every instruction before she gave it and would comply with a beautiful synergistic trust. His white mane and tail billowed magnificently on the air as he carried her through the farm.

Millie was on tenterhooks aboard Candesco. She knew where the car was going. Could she reach him in time? With her heart thrumming in her chest and her nerves jangling, she urged pony on into the woodland beyond the sheep fields. Ducking branches and hurtling between trees, Millie directed the pony through many a twist and turn along the earthen track.

"Sirens! The police are close. Come on, Candesco!" Millie gave a slight squeeze of her knees and the smallest right tug on her reins.

Candesco lifted his head with a determined neigh. Sending earth flying from his hooves, he jinked right and leapt the rhododendron hedge. As leaves hit the ground, he thundered out of the trees onto the dirt track road.

Millie's strong amber eyes locked on the red three-door hatchback car barrelling towards her. She knew it was the kidnapper's car. The pursuing police vehicle was right behind but losing ground. Millie knew to stop him would put her in danger but she had to try. "We need to head him off, Candesco. Let's go!" Leaning forward she held rein and mane as she was whipped through the air.

Candesco had anticipated his mistress, he galloped left into a field through an open gate. The car missed him by less than the tails width. He flared his nostrils angrily but powered on across the potato furrows to please his mistress.

Millie forced her ponytail from her face as she looked over her shoulder. The police car was struggling over rough ground. She knew the kidnapper would regain the tarmac roads and disappear before it could catch him. "We have one chance with this – trust me, sweet Candesco." Millie patted his heaving, warm flanks and urged him on.

Candesco nodded his head in full understanding. He angled straight for the far gate.

Millie flicked her gaze between the gate and the splashes of red she could see racing along the hedge line. "Faster, Candesco!"

Candesco complied, lowering his head and streamlining his body as he galloped on in a fury of flying earth, potatoes and terrified pigeons.

Millie's world became a blur as the gate and car grew closer. She locked her focus upon the two and held on with her hands and knees. "Candesco, NOW!"

The pony let out a nicker and threw himself into the air.

Millie shrieked like a grey streak of lightning, Candesco flew over the gate. Everything seemed to slow as his hooves thundered onto the bonnet of the kidnapper's car. The windscreen glass shattered and then the pony was airborne again, flying over a second gate and landing neatly in another field.

On the pony's back, Millie punched the air in delight. "We did it!" she yelled amid the car's brakes screeching as it crunched sideways into the hedge. She turned Candesco and trotted him sedately out of the field and put him in front of the car. "Good boy my sweet, Candesco. Look at the hoof marks in the bonnet, you nailed it good!" She remarked while admiring her handiwork at turning the car into a smoking wreck.

The driver's door opened revealing a man wearing jeans and a dirty leather jacket. His nose was bleeding into his stubbly beard. Millie reckoned his head must have struck the steering wheel when he crashed.

"What the hell! Now, I'll bloody kidnap you too!" yelled the man.

Millie gripped Candesco's mane. "Stay where you are or I'll have him kick you!" she warned as the pony flared his nostrils and pawed the ground.

The man drew a knife. "No chance, I'll cut his head off first!" He lunged causing the light to glint upon the edge of his keen blade.

"Well, we warned you," Millie felt Candesco's muscles tense beneath her. He reared high, kicking the kidnapper in the wrist. The knife flew from his hand as the pony drove him to the ground and pinned him beneath a hoof.

"Argh! The horse is killing me. Get off me now!" screamed the man writhing and unable to escape from beneath a large pony.

Millie slipped gracefully down from Candesco's back and grinned at him. "He's a pony actually!" Sticking her tongue out, she added, "You look comfortable down there to me. You can stay put until the police come. Hold him, Candesco." She grinned victoriously as she waved to the police car trundling like a lame cow along the lane.

"No, let me go!" demanded the man.

Millie ignored him and went to the still smoking car. She leant into the open door and smiled at the girl in the back. She was maybe seven and had on a pink dress and

54

blonde pigtails. "Hi, you can come out now. I'm Millie. Candesco and I saved you."

The little girl had been crying, but now she was smiling with tears still glistening on her cheeks and wonderment in her powder-blue eyes. "Y-you were riding the pony?"

Millie nodded and held out her hand. "Yes, come and meet him."

"Thank you. That jump was amazing!" The little girl took the offered hand. "I'm Natasha but daddy calls me Natty. Mummy doesn't like him doing that," she explained as she clambered out between the seats.

Millie grinned. "I wonder why? Natty sounds cute."

"I agree," said a police officer coming over. "I'm glad to see you're okay, Natasha. Your mummy and daddy have been worried about you."

The little girl began to cry. "I want my mummy and daddy!"

Millie put an arm around her. "We'll get you back to them very soon, I promise."

"We sure will, little one." The officer ruffled her pigtails drawing a smile then focused on Millie. "That was some epic riding, Miss. However, I must ask you to get your pony off my suspect so I can arrest him."

Millie giggled. "Of course, officer. Candesco won't hurt you, don't worry." She whistled and smiled expectantly at the pony.

Candesco nickered and made the kidnapper scream as he removed his hoof and stepped right over him to his mistress's side.

"What a wonderful, fellow," the officer remarked as he went to make his arrest.

"Thank you, Officer." Millie smiled proudly as she handed Natasha the reins. "There, you hold him and we'll walk him back together."

55

Natasha looked a little scared of the much larger pony but she held the reins anyway. "Thank you, I never been this close to a pony before."

"Well, I think you deserve a treat after your kidnapping," said the officer, now holding the fuming kidnapper in handcuffs. "But you can't stay with him long. We have to get you home."

Millie nodded in agreement while smoothing the pony's silky snout. "Yeah, we do. Candesco and I live at Coney Farm. Why not bring her parents there?"

"Yes, please, please!" begged Natasha.

"I think that's a good idea," said the officer putting the kidnapper in his car with a smile at the girls. "You go on ahead, I'll arrange it over the radio."

"That's great, thank you," said Millie.

And so Millie took Natasha to the farm where she met the sheep and the rest of the ponies and had a wonderful time until her parents came to collect her. Millie was branded a hero; she and Candesco were awarded medals for their heroic rescue. And from that day on Millie always listened to the police radio in the hope that she could ride to the rescue once more.

Gold Fall

" 'Ey, Jack! We gotta problem down 'ere!" Eric's voice echoed along the mine tunnel. The headlamp of his friend and partner began bobbing towards him in the dull orangey light.

"What's up, mate?" Jack called. At almost six-and-a-half-feet tall, he had to bend to walk along the tunnel.

"I think we 'ave to stop chasing this 'ere seam of gold. Listen." Eric swung his pick into the quartz. Each blow causing a shower of rock and sparks. More concerning, the impacts seem to foment hollow rumbles and knocks within the strata.

Jack swore. "Yup, sounds like you're waking up the Tommyknockers and that's never a good sign."

Both men stood listening, each well aware of the legend of the Tommyknockers. The impish leprechaun like creatures were supposed to be mischievous with miners equipment. They'd also act as a warning with their knocking telling of imminent cave-ins.

"What you reckon? Stop completely or dynamite it?"

"There's too much gold to lose here. Get some dyna—" Another series of knocks echoed along the tunnel. The wall holding the gold vein began to split as a rumbling shook the mine.

"Shit!" Eric dropped his pickaxe and backed away. Large chunks of rock began to fall from the ceiling. He made it two feet before a loud bang rocked the underground space.

"That's it! Get out! We have to let the mine rid itself of pressure!" Jack yelled.

"Just run!" Eric watched him turn and felt his stomach drop. The floor of the tunnel had given way. Both men were slammed on their backs and sent tumbling into a dark abyss.

The miners had become human rocks in an underground

landslide. Both cried out as their bodies were assaulted by falling boulders, hard surfaces and rubble.

Eric heard his partner scream in pain as he plunged into an area of cold air. There was no time to react as he somersaulted into space. His headlamp gave him a fleeting glance of a grey lake as he plunged into icy-cold water. All around him boulders and debris splashed down like the most horrendous hailstorm.

Hitting the bottom of the lake, he instinctively kicked up and away from danger. He swam strongly until his head broke the surface. Gasping for air, he felt his heart racing as his body tried to cope with the sudden icy immersion. Mercifully his helmet light had survived so he could see. "Ja-ck! J-ack where are ya!" He yelled, his voice echoing around the cavern.

The lake was in a subterranean room with no way out. Its walls made of yellow and brown rock – sandstone or something similar. The ceiling was hanging with hundreds of long thin stalactites giving the feeling of being in the mouth of a giant monster.

"Jack!" Eric saw a flat sandy area and swam for that. He felt a sense of great relief as he hauled himself out to relative safety.

"Eric, help!"

The echoic voice was shallow and full of fear. "I'm coming mate. 'old on!" Eric hauled himself to his feet. His limbs chest and back felt as if they'd been pummelled by a world champion kickboxer.

"Over here," Jack swore through some pain.

Eric spotted a little light coming from the newly formed boulder field. Having no intention of getting in the lake again, he began to pick his way around the shore. The going was treacherous on the slippery rocks. "Jack, there you are. You okay, mate?" He'd mounted a large boulder to discover his friend lying in the rubble.

"No, my arm's stuck. It's bloody broken." Jack was white with pain and trembling.

"Is that all? It's all right for you. I fell in the bleeding drink. It was bloody freezing, let me tell you!" Eric said with a chuckle.

Jack managed a laugh but it was strangled out by a wave of pain leaving him choking. "You needed a bath anyway," he wheezed.

"Yup, the missus will be happy." Eric dropped down beside his friend. His light told him the bad news. The offending boulder had crashed down on his forearm. *Shit, this must be five tons,* he thought while looking about for a way to move it.

"Don't sugar-coat nothing. How bad is it?"

"I'll get you out, Jack. Don't worry."

"Ah, bloody hell… Look, forget me. You try to get out. Maybe you can bring back help. Either way, no sense us both dying—"

"Jack?"

"Yeah."

"Shut yer face!" Eric took his good hand and grasp it tight. "I'm not leaving yer, mate. I'll get yer free and we'll get out of 'ere together, alright?"

Tears formed and flowed down Jack's dirty cheeks. "That means more than you know my, friend. Please promise me; if you can't free me – get out I need somebody to tell my wife I love her. To ensure she and Daisy are well taken care of."

" 'Ey, I met your wife remember. I ain't telling 'er nothing. If I leave you down 'ere she'll kill me anyway." Eric stood up. "No, you can tell 'er yourself later. 'Old on a minute. I'll see if I can find my pickaxe."

"Thanks, Eric. You're a good, Pal."

"Only doing what you'd do for me." Eric mantled

another boulder and scanned the debris field. It took him ten minutes to find his pickaxe and make another discovery. " 'Oly Midas, Jack!" he yelled causing his voice echo in the cavern.

"Gah, did you have to bloody shout!" Jack called back from beneath his boulder.

"You bet I did." Eric chiselled at the wall beneath the rockfall for a moment. "Look at this!" he said once back by Jack's side. In his hand was a sizeable chunk of quartz sparkling with heavy gold deposits. "There's a shitload of this over there."

Jack's eyes went wide. "Haha! Jackpot. Hurry up and get me out of this so we can get rich."

"Might 'ave to leave you down 'ere after all," Eric replied with a sinister look on his face.

Jack gulped turning greyer as a moribund feeling of fear descended upon him.

Eric burst into laughter. "Just kidding, mate. All this gold would be no fun if I couldn't share it with you."

"Arsehole! You scared the shit out of me. I'll belt you when I get up!" Jack grumbled as a wave of pain twisted his features.

"Speaking of which." Eric began chopping away at the rock and debris around his friend's trapped arm. He knew we couldn't move the boulder and so wasn't going to try. Instead, he methodically worked to free him from below.

Almost an hour passed before Jack was able to sit up. His hand and arm were purple from being trapped for so long. His forearm bones and wrist without doubt broken. "Looks like I'll be a silent partner from here on out. I can't work a pickaxe with this hand anymore," he said overcome by sadness.

"You silent. Ha, no chance. You never shut up!" Eric

chuckled as he withdrew a folding knife from his jacket pocket. He levered the business end from his pickaxe. Next, he used the blade to carve long strips from the handle.

"I don't know what you're doing. But I'm glad, I'm trapped down here with you. I couldn't have survived with anybody else," Eric said cradling his arm against his chest.

"Likewise, partner. Let's see that arm." Eric had pulled his bootlaces out. He placed the strips of wood along Jack's shattered forearm and secured them with the laces. Every time he applied pressure the poor man screamed in pain. "This is only a makeshift splinting but it might help save your arm until we can get you to hospital."

"That... was... genius," Jack panted, his body close to collapse through the pain. "Now, how do we get out? I don't think I can climb back up there."

Eric eyed the hole they'd fallen through. "No, we can't go that way." He put his head under Jack's good arm and helped him stand. "We'll try down there and hope our luck holds."

Alongside the gold vein, a crack in the wall opened into the hidden passage. The miners knew by the smooth walls it had been made by running water. Probably that which once fed the lake. They were forced to stop at short intervals to allow Jack to catch his breath. Finding a smaller underground room with a sandy floor, they lay down to sleep, both overcome with exhaustion from the crazy day.

Hours later, neither man knew whether it was day or night in the dark caverns. Eric woke determined to get his friend to the hospital soon. By then both their lamps had run out of oil.

"We're done for. We can't get out in the dark," Jack groaned.

"You can still get your arse up. Come on!" Eric hauled

him to his feet and marched him forward. Using his hands on the walls to guide them down the tunnel.

Immeasurable time vanished in the darkness. The greatest sight for any miner appeared ahead – daylight. The miners broke free of the tunnels, entering into a rocky valley below the mine.

"We did it! You saved me, Eric!" Jack said tearfully as they hugged awkwardly on account of his arm.

"Any time, my friend. Let's get you healing and us rich!" Eric beamed as they began to walk around to their vehicles. It would take Jack months to heal. Even then he'd never get full mobility of his hand back. The two friends enlisted a young lad from the village. Between the three, they were soon the owners a substantial pile of gold. Something, I'm sure the Tommyknockers were not very pleased about.

Grandmother's Last Gift

I stood at the back of the choir, miming as usual. Quintin the choirmaster made me nervous. I was too scared to let my voice out, but deep inside I wanted the world to hear it. I internally begged for one chance to show everyone how good I could be.

The choirmaster stood conducting like an emperor penguin in his tailed suit and little glasses. His gaze flicked up to me with all the intensity of a suspicious owl. He knew I was lip-synching. I'd be in for an ear-bashing later.

Swallowing my fear brought me close to choking through my parchment dry mouth. I could do this; opening my mouth to sing for real, I hid a grin. The song came to an end just then. Now, I could snooze while the next act performed. Gazing into my candle, I allowed the room to become nothing more than a blur as the audience applauded.

"Wasn't that beautiful ladies and gentlemen," began headmaster Wallace Gordon taking to the stage. "Next up we have a soloist who's going to delight us with his enchanting voice. Ladies and gentlemen, give it up for Jez Beckett!"

The audience broke into polite applause.

Meanwhile, I dissolved into total shock. That was my name! I hadn't put myself up to sing a solo. Somebody was setting me up. I couldn't perform with the choir, forget singing alone!

"Well, Mr Beckett. The stage is yours." Gordon focused on me.

I saw the spotlight shining on his bald head. A series of red marks indicated his skull had met door frames more times than he'd care to admit. Meeting his eyes, I stood frozen to my spot in the choirstall.

"Mr Beckett?"

"I…" My candle blew out. There was no breeze in the room and yet the flame had flicked sharply to the right on a mercurial gust before extinguishing.

"Jez, wake up!"

My feet must've leapt three feet off the floor. Quintin had appeared right beside me scaring the living daylights out of me. "Sorry, I…" Fingertips in my hair. I could feel somebody caressing my hair! I glanced at Amy beside me. Her hands were clasped about her candle. She was glaring at me – a look unsuiting her pretty face. I wished she would smile. Lord knows I love her! Still, nobody could be touching me!

"Jez! Get on the stage. Do not screw this performance up!" Quintin demanded.

The hand smoothed my hair again, filling my body with cold static electricity. "I didn't—" something pressed against my belly stealing the words from my tongue.

Jez, darling. Sing. Sing like an angel. The female voice seemed inhuman. It seemed to belong to the invisible breeze circling me.

"You did what?" Quintin scowled at me over his glasses.

Pressure against my back, pushing me from my place in the choir. I stumbled past Quintin and almost fell down the steps.

"Ladies and gentlemen, Jez Beckett," announced headmaster Gordon to fresh applause.

Reaching the bottom of the steps, I cut in front of my friends in the choir. Glancing back towards my place, I caught sight of a spectral figure beside Amy. A woman in a white dress, scarcely brighter than the tree mural upon the wall. I knew who she was.

The ghost nodded to me, *Yes, my boy. Sing. Show everyone that beautiful voice you possess.*

"I will, Grandmother," I whispered to myself as I approached the microphone. Then it hit me. What was I supposed to be singing? I hadn't planned to do this at all. I had no idea which song the orchestra had been given for me. It filled me with dread. Looking at the sea of mums, dads, students and teachers enhanced it to a point where my feet started to demand I ran away. Yet I couldn't – I had to do this!"

The drummer kicked in first, then the guitarists, violins, flutes. Finally, the pianist and the melody – my melody.

This was a song I composed a while ago. Nobody should have known it existed; let alone have the music sheet and be playing it in a live show without my permission. A knot of fury and fear twisted my stomach There was another problem too!

I took a deep breath and glanced back up at the choir stalls. Time to commit reputational suicide.

"Floor's yours, Mr Beckett," said Mr Symons the orchestra conductor.

"*Rock it, my boy!*" added my grandmother so close I could smell the violets of her perfume.

Taking a deep breath, I closed my eyes and curled my sweating, shaking hands around the microphone.

♫ *Down by the sea*
  Just you and me
  Here we are
  Waltzing on the sandbar ♫

I felt the ripple of applause from the audience more than I heard it. They'd enjoyed the first stanza. It was this next bit, the chorus, where the trouble was coming. Still, I opened my mouth and sang with all my heart and soul.

65

♫ *Amy – do you love me*
Amy – set my heart free
You are my shining star
Waltzing on the sandbar ♫

I heard her gasp from the choir stalls as the audience's hearts melted. I was committed now. I'd finish what I started and then run like hell.

♫ *White horses on the tide*
I hug you to my side
You play my heart's guitar
Waltzing on the sandbar ♫

As the orchestra ramped up the music, I couldn't hear a murmur from anyone. I could only hope that meant they were enchanted by my soulful ballad.

♫ *Amy – know I love you*
Amy – my pretty honeydew
You are my caviar
Waltzing on the sandbar ♫

One final chorus to sing. Should I stay or should I run? For now, I opened my mouth and sang my ballad to its powerful end.

♫ *Amy – do you love me*
Amy – set my heart free
You are my shining star
Waltzing on the sandbar ♫

As my words died away, I stood breathing heavily, feeling the sweat from the spotlight running down my face. Then they did it, the audience erupted into applause and whistles.

"Ladies and gentlemen, I give you, Jez Beckett!" announced headmaster Gordon.

I bowed to another round of applause. "Thank you," I said into the microphone before walking away along the front of the choir – a trembling mess.

"Well done, my boy. You showed everyone you deserve to be number one in the charts," said my grandmother's spirit. I saw her up by the tree mural again. With a wave, she faded away through the wall.

"Up next, Jez will be singing with the choir as they perform the classic hymn *Sunshine!*"

Well, now, I had to retake my place beside Amy in the choir. The next thing the audience would hear, was her slapping my face into oblivion.

Tripping up the steps, I walked into my position and took up my candle, without looking toward Amy. Even so, I could feel her boring a hole into my skull with her pretty dark eyes.

"Hey, popstar," she said as the orchestra struck up again.

I glanced her way trying to gauge her reaction as I counted down the notes to begin to sing again. I registered shock and teary eyes, what was she thinking?

"Jez, am I the Amy in your song?"

Gulping, I decided to say nothing. My preference was to get beaten to a pulp out of the view of everyone.

"You did sing that for me, didn't you?" Amy prodded as everyone began to sing.

I nodded as I mouthed the words for the first stanza – too nervous to sing again.

"Just know, I'd waltz on the beach any day with you." Amy reached over and kissed my cheek.

As the second stanza began, I took a deep breath. I opened my mouth and sang with a smile on my face.

My grandmother died several years ago. How she'd gotten me and my song into the show I'd never know. But I'd be eternally grateful for the gift she'd given me. Especially, as I got to finish the show hand-in-hand with Amy.

Hartley's Fantasy

Hartley picked her way through rubble, plaster dust and old, peeled paint chippings to reach her favourite window. This used to be a five-storey block of apartments until inspectors came and said it was subsiding. They'd condemned the building when Hartley was seven. If subsiding meant collapsing, this building was an exception to the rule. She was nineteen now and although it was in a state of dilapidation the building was still standing.

Family life had always been difficult for Hartley. Daily arguments, money issues and beatings for no reason. This building had become a refuge for her over the years. She'd explored every room and floor and knew its deepest secrets. In the last few weeks, something had changed right outside her favourite window on the fourth floor.

The glass was long gone and so she leant at the peeling, chipped frame to peer outside. Silvery grey clouds floated lazily over the green hillside. Casting her eyes to the scene below, Hartley saw the trenches of the archaeological dig. Each measured about six-feet-square showing the importance of the dig.

The rugged, handsome gentleman in the cream shirt and jeans was Dale Dawson the leading archaeologist. He was in control the six other men and women down there today. Hartley watched him drip water down his shirt as he drank from his bottle. She longed to run down there – not to kiss him, although that would be nice too – but to tell him the secrets she knew.

Hartley had read about the dig in the papers and followed the story on social media. She knew they were digging in the remains of the old castle in the hope of discovering the treasures it once held. The basic truth was, they were digging in the wrong place. Should she run down there and tell them? No, they'd likely mob her until she left and tell her not to interfere with the dig. That was the trouble with being a teenage girl in the dainty black dress which showed her dirty knees. Nobody ever believed anything she had to say. Hartley let out a sigh and perched on the sill to watch the men work. She longed to run down there and make Dale's dream come true.

A rain shower blew through and then the sun came out as the day wore on. Hartley grew hungry after a time. She tore her eyes from Dale and picked her way to the stairs. When she reached the ground floor, she paused to stroke Whiskers the cat. He was feral and had lived there about as long as Hartley could remember. She straightened herself and smoothed her long blonde hair over her shoulder and stepped into the foyer. Somebody was standing there. She gasped and made a run for the nearest door.

"Hey! There's no need to run. Who are you?" he called to her.

Hartley froze, almost hugging the doorframe – could she trust him? "I'm Hartley. I have a secret I think you'd like to know." She gave a bashful look over her shoulder and felt her heart rate increase. It was the archaeologist, standing right there. Smiling at her.

"I don't doubt that for a second. I'm Dale. I run the dig out there," he gestured with a strong forearm. "What's a pretty lady like you doing in this desolate old building?"

Taking a deep breath, Hartley unfurled herself from the door frame and gave a coy smile as she took a measured step toward him. "This old place has been my home from home and hiding place for years."

"Really? You'll be sorry to hear they're going to demolish it to build a new apartment complex soon, then." Dale's eyes wandered over her with admiring quality about them.

Hartley felt the heat rising in her cheeks. He seemed to like her; she didn't think anybody would ever feel that way toward her. "I'd heard that, but hoped it wouldn't happen. You'll never find what you're looking for if they do that."

"Oh?" Dale scratched his handsome chin while giving her a quizzical look. "What am I searching for then?"

Me hopefully! Hartley thought while hiding a wry smile. "You're searching for the legendary vault in the Castle and its five chests of treasure."

Dale's mouth dropped open. "And you know where it is?"

Hartley nodded and grinned.

"Will you show me?"

Hartley shook her head – teasing him.

Dale put his hands together before him. "Please."

"Okay, since you begged so nicely." Hartley skipped forward and took his hand. "Come on!"

"Hey, what's the rush?"

Hartley just smiled, she felt like she was whisking her prince away. She led him back past the steps to the upper floors and around behind them. Here an old door hung off the hinges. It squeaked as she pushed it aside and ducked inside.

Hartley shuddered as she entered a spooky basement room. "There look. This basement was built right alongside the old castle foundations. I think that wall collapsing is why they condemned this building. It wasn't subsidence though; there's a room behind there." Hartley aimed her light towards a pile of crumbled masonry and a cave like crack going deep into the wall.

Dale freed himself of Hartley, took his phone from his back pocket, and moved closer to have a look. "Wow! I wish you'd come and told us about this sooner."

"I thought you'd all mob me for trespassing if I came.

Maybe have me arrested because I interfered." Hartley confessed.

The archaeologist smiled at her. "Do I really seem that officious to you?"

Hartley shook her head and blushed while avoiding his gaze. "No – go and look inside!"

"Okay." Dale cautiously stepped inside with Hartley right behind him. The brownstone walls in here were centuries older. There is no doubt this was the castle dungeon. There was even iron sconces and rings for shackling prisoners still in the walls.

"Over there to the right," Hartley directed while staying back. "I'm sure that's your vault even though I couldn't get it open." She watched the archaeologist approach a solid-looking wrought-iron studded oak door. It had an arched top which seemed to secure it to the stone walls.

"This is incredible!" Dale ran his hands over the door and gave handle a solid tug.

"It has funny ancient padlocked bolts."

"So, it does." Dale smiled at Hartley. "This is so exciting!" The archaeologist returned to the basement opening and selected a sizeable brick. "Stand back," he warned as he struck the first padlock with a thunderous bang.

"Going for a nice gentle approach, I see," Hartley said with a giggle.

"Always." Dale winked and continued to work. Sweat beaded his brow before he managed to get the locks off. Then with a flex of his muscles, he yanked the heavy door open.

Hartley felt tingly with anticipation as she watched him enter.

"Haha! Hartley, you beauty! Just look at this!" He yelled moments later.

She ran inside and broke into a triumphant smile. The

room wasn't large but big enough to contain five ornate treasure chests. Each gold-leafed and adorned with jewels. Dale had opened one revealing even more golden riches inside. "Oh, it's incredible!" Hartley felt herself go teary-eyed it was so overwhelming.

"No, you're incredible!" Dale turned to face her, his eyes meeting hers in an impassioned gaze. "I mean, this is your discovery. I just helped you access it."

"Thank you for trusting me enough to come and see. I…" Hartley became silent as she watched him take a queen's crown from the chest. Glittering with emeralds and rubies it was magnificent. As he placed it in her hair she was filled with regal energy and enchanted by his smile.

"Thank you for trusting me enough to share it with me. Hartley, I…"

She watched him take a deep breath and look away. "What is it? What's wrong, Dale?"

"I er— I have a confession to make. I wasn't just exploring when I entered the building. I was looking for you. I've seen you watching me for a few days now and well… you bewitched me with your pretty dresses and silky hair. I wanted to meet you to know who you were and…" Dale reached in and kissed her.

Hartley stood wide-eyed with shock, *He loves me!* Shaking herself back to reality, she kissed him back for a long blissful moment. "Dale, what does this mean?"

"Let's reveal your treasure to the world and find out."

Honestly Deceiving

Old Edgar looked like a contented artist at his easel beneath the spire of the cathedral. With his cloth cap on his head of white hair, a spattered apron covering his shirt and trousers, and a paintbrush in his hand; he looked the part. He'd positioned himself on the busy footpath earlier in the day. Now, he was adding a little detail here and there.

"That's pretty good," said a lady coming to a stop to admire his work.

"Thank ya, darlin'. Been painting a lot a years, I have." Edgar dropped his eyes to her bag – open at the top – perfect.

"It shows. You get so much detail in your work."

"You see, it's a case a doing it in layers." Edgar's hand removed her purse from the bag. "I put the background in first an' then I lay in the buildin' like this…" he indicated his painting with his paintbrush while removing the ladies bank card. He swiped it over his pocket, put it back in the purse and returned it to her bag. "… Then I go back in an' add the fine detail here and there with a liner brush to finish."

"Remarkable. Thank you for explaining."

"My pleasure, darlin'. You have a lovely day." Edgar let her go and continued adding shades of grey to his stonework.

"Excuse me, mate, I'm guessing you know the area well?" said a man in a suit not ten minutes later.

"Sort a, yeah. Where ya tryin' ta get to?" Edgar's scanned his eyes over the gentleman and refocused on his painting.

"Train station. I know's around here somewhere." The gentleman gazed about him and scratched his head.

"Ah, ya not far, sir. Be easier if I could show ya on a map."

"Good idea. I got one on my phone." The gentleman retrieved a new iPhone from his inside pocket.

Edgar watched him put the code in and smiled a toothy grin. "That's a smart-looking bit a new-fangled kit ya got there."

"For eight hundred quid it better be good." The man found the map and waited for the GPS to locate him. "Okay, says we're here."

Edgar pulled his glasses case from his pocket and spilt it on the floor. He scrambled to get them and tumbled off his seat. "Blast my old age!"

"Here, let me help you." The gentleman offered a hand.

Edgar took his hand at the wrist, a quick twist as he stood up and he had the gentleman's watch away. "So, sorry about that. Thank ya, for yer help."

"Of course. Are you, okay?" The gentleman looked quite concerned as he gave Edgar his glasses.

"I'm fine. Now, then." Edgar focused on the phone. "This is the train station, here. If ya go along the road that way and through the alleyway marked there. You come out on Prince a Wales road – it's just down on your left then."

"That's great, thank you." The gentleman slipped his phone in his outside pocket and reached to shake Edgar's hand.

"My pleasure, now don't forget..." Edgar shook the man's hand and then pointed away down the road, his other hand going into the man's pocket and relieving him of his phone. "... Go along here and through the alley; it's just beyond the building with the purple buddleia along there. Alright?"

"Thanks again, mate. Enjoy your painting."

Edgar smiled. The second the gentleman turned to leave; he took the stolen phone out. He slipped a USB stick into the charging point and grinned as the phone unlocked.

He pressed a few keys and scanned a QR code on his easel. Deception complete, he stood to a called, "Sir."

"Something wrong?" said the gentleman coming back.

"I couldn't do it. While we were talkin', I took yer phone. Oh, and your watch. You helped me an' so I can't deceive you of them. Here ya go. I'm sorry." Edgar returned the items.

"Huh, an honest thief. Who'd have thought it." The gentleman gave a wistful smile and walked away shaking his head.

By dusk, Edgar had worked his larceny a good many times. He packed up his things and wandered away whistling to himself. He walked to the bank and put a card in the ATM. When it showed him the account balance, he grinned.

The account had been empty this morning and now after a day of scanning phones and triggering contactless payments on debit cards, it contained over three hundred pounds. He withdrew the lot and closed the account. He'd always make a new account each day at different banks and then simply create dummy cards to operate them.

Edgar left the bank and walked to a large building not too far away and knocked on the door.

"Hallo, Edgar. The kids have been waiting on you," said a kindly-looking lady answering the door.

"Nice ta see ya, Julie." Edgar smiled at the "Bure Valley Orphanage" sign as he entered. He left his painting things in the hall and entered a large room. It was set like a classroom. A group of thirty children were sitting in a circle singing a pop song with a guardian Edgar knew to be called Tom.

"Look, kids. Edgar came to see you," said Julie.

The kids cheered like he was Santa Claus. Some even ran to hug him.

"Hi, kids." Edgar beamed; he loved this part of his day.

He took his day's money from his pocket and gave every child a fair share. "You all, put that away for when you really need it, okay?"

"Thank you, Mr Edgar," they chimed.

"Are we having a story?" asked a little boy.

Edgar nodded and sat down cross-legged on the floor. He patted the floor beside him for the boy to join him. "Once upon a time…"

Incident at Pixie Falls

"Listen up, team! We have a small waterfall up ahead. Beyond that, we'll drop into a smoother current and find a place to pull out for dinner," Granger yelled over the roaring white water that churned beneath the yellow inflatable raft.

"Heard, captain!" replied five of the six rafters.

"Bess, are you with us?" Granger tapped the girl on the shoulder. She was so lost in gazing at the banks whizzing by, she wasn't even rowing with the others.

"Hey, Bess. Wake up!" said her friend Dave.

"Oops sorry! I was mesmerised by all the beautiful red bell-shaped flowers along the banks. It's just so pretty over there."

"No harm done. Those are rhododendrons. They're rainforest shrubs. See how they choke out all the native plants here?" Granger explained with his deep green eyes focused on the river ahead. "Still, they are lovely to look at during spring."

"Thank you for telling me." Beth smiled as she began paddling again.

Granger gave her a wink then pulled on his paddle. "Here comes the rough and falls! Stay in sync everybody. Paddle as one. Keep to the centre of the river."

The raft dropped into a depression, then lunged into a crest. Its passengers squealed in delight. Everybody paddled hard and fought to stay aboard.

"This is amazing!" yelled Dave.

"And terrifying!" Bess replied, red in the face from the cold water.

"Paddles aft! Rocks ahead!" Granger ordered.

The team dug in, turning the raft away into the flow. Battered by the white water, it careened around the glistening teeth-like rocks.

Bess felt her paddle strike the obstacle. It threatened to tear from her hands but she hung on gamely.

The raft gained speed and bucked like a donkey as the river put it through a rapid spin cycle.

"Wooo! It's not so Baaa—" Dave spluttered as he was hit clean in the face by a wall of water.

Everyone burst out laughing as they clung to the rocking and rolling vessel.

"Don't drink up the river, old boy. There will be a long hike from here!" Remarked Ian; another of the team.

His partner Lisa opened her mouth to speak but was drowned out.

"Get centred! Paddle hard, keep left, prepare to drop into the falls!" Granger yelled. His strong voice was hoarse from issuing his commands.

"Stroke! Stroke! Stroke!" Chorused the team, digging hard into the water. Forcing the raft to comply with them over the water.

Then there was no water, just froth and vapour as the river drops beneath the raft.

The air was filled with screams of fear and excitement. The air boomed with the roaring water.

"Hold on tight!" yelled Granger.

The raft splashed down with a mighty slap. It seemed to burrow into the water, only to rebound back into the light.

"We made it!" yelled Lisa now dripping wet.

"Not quite. Everyone, hard alee!" Granger shouted. Flexing his strong arms he yelled for the team to haul the raft ashore.

It was then Bess realised. "Dave!"

"We'll find him, Bess." Granger had the team beach the raft on a sandbank a hundred yards from the waterfall. "Everyone, stop down and begin dinner."

"Nothing doing; we'll walk downstream and check for Dave there," Ian said without a second thought.

"Thank you. Bess, with me." Granger unzipped his buoyancy aid and strode through the rhododendrons back towards the waterfall.

"Should we call for rescue?" Bess asked looking at the churning water.

"We will, but we'll have a scrat around first." Granger indicated the rock wall. "Let's climb up and take a look."

Bess watched the weather-worn team leader dig his hands and feet into the crevices and climb the ten feet with ease. Taking a deep breath, she followed suit and used the same holds, he did.

"You climb well," Granger said with a smile as the two scoured the river atop the waterfall.

"Thank you." Bess blushed. "Look!" She ran to the riverbank, and pulled a broken paddle from between the rocks.

"Good spot. I bet that's how Dave was thrown from the boat." Granger scratched his stubbly chin with a graveness weighting his brows. "Let's go back down. If these rocks threw him, he went over the falls."

"I was thinking the same thing." Bess wiped her eyes and lowered her head as they trooped back. She had a horrible feeling her best friend was dead.

Regaining the sandbank, they returned to the raft. The others hadn't returned yet so there was nothing to do but wait.

Granger took out his radio. "Requesting, search and rescue. One man lost at the Pixie Falls." Hearing only static he repeated his message then listened.

"Message received. Rescue team en route!" came a reply moments later.

"Roger that!" Granger walked toward the woods. "I'll get firewood. Back shortly."

Bess nodded and dropped into a sitting position,

hugging her knees. David had brought her on this trip because she begged him to. Now it seemed she'd gotten him killed.

Time lost all meaning as she waited in silence.

"Err, Bess – Look!" Granger yelled having reappeared with a bundle of branches over a shoulder.

Bess flinched and looked. The rest of the team had returned with Ian and Lisa leading the way. Just beyond them was Dave.

He looked like he'd lost the war but was smiling. More than that his arms were filled with the great red bells of the rhododendron flowers.

"Dave! Oh, Dave, you're alive!" Bess squealed as she bounded to her feet and ran to him.

"I'm okay. I have a few bruises, but I'm fine," he told her.

Bess threw her arms around him. "You scared me so much!"

"I'm sorry. Look." Dave handed her the flowers. "You said these are beautiful right?"

Bess nodded.

"Good, they must have been nurtured in your image. Because you're beautiful too."

"What?" Bess gaped as she smelled the flowers.

"I'm saying, that nearly drowning reminded me of why I agreed to come with you. I didn't do that because we're friends. I did that because I love spending time with you." Dave leaned in and kissed her.

Bess kissed back. "I love spending time with you too."

"Jolly good!" Granger said. "I've called off the rescue. Let's have a dinner party to celebrate!"

"Here, here!" yelled everyone.

Bess sat beside Dave and placed her head against his chest.

Granger beamed at them. Rafting always brought people closer together. That was why he loved the extreme sport so much.

Interview Intervention

Tamsin's heart drummed frantically as she tore through her pack, her books, and the messy desk– where was it? Her interview was within an hour and she had no hope of securing her precious job without that recommendation letter.

"Tamsin, you're going to be late!" called her mother.

"Yes, I know! Can't find my bloody letter!" she replied with a groan in her voice.

"The one from Doctor Felix?"

"Yeah, that one." Tamsin, threw everything back in her bag, resigning herself to having to take the interview without it.

"It's here. You pinned it on the notice board for safekeeping, remember." Mother brought it through. "Here, look. Take it and vamoose – and good luck!"

"Phew, thanks, Mum!" Tamsin kissed her on the cheek, put the letter in her folder and left at a run.

Outside she jumped in her lime-green Ford Ka and set off toward the hospital.

The Norfolk and Norwich Hospital bordered the leafy landscape of the University Park. Tamsin felt herself relaxing in the natural surroundings as she drove towards her interview. If successful she would promote herself from triage nurse to surgery nurse. She had successfully completed all the training and now needed the job she'd work so hard for.

An ambulance turned right at the roundabout ahead. Tamsin indicated to follow. Somebody raced in front of her car waving frantically. She slammed on the brakes causing the tyres to shriek on the tarmac. Somehow she brought her little car to a controlled stop an inch from disaster. "What on earth were you thinking!" she yelled out of the window.

"Please, help! He collapsed," yelled a teenage boy.

"Who collapsed? Where?" Tamsin pulled the car off the road and got out. Now she could tell the boy was a football player going by his shorts and t-shirt.

"Rico, he's on the sidelines of the football pitch."

'Shit, Now I'll really miss my interview!' Tamsin thought. "Okay, lead me to him. Have you called an ambulance?"

"This way and my phone's not working." The boy set off running across the field.

Tamsin followed with her phone to her ear. "This is nurse Tamsin Wellesley. Requesting an ambulance to attend the University Park football pitch... I'll give you more details when I reach the patient..."

"Hurry up!" yelled the boy, his voice filled with panic.

Tamsin saw a prone figure ahead not far from the red corner flag on the pitch sidelines. Another footballer was leaning over him along with a girl wearing shorts and a crop top. As soon as she reached them, Tamsin knew the boy was not well. "What happened guys?" She asked while dropping to her knees beside him.

"He went to take a throw-in and collapsed," said the girl tearfully.

"Don't worry we'll help him." Tamsin lifted her phone. "Despatcher, I've got a teenage boy. He's not breathing. I have no pulse. Beginning CPR."

"Received, ambulance five minutes away," replied the dispatcher on the phone.

Tamsin dropped the device and set herself to the task. Having cleared his airway, she began rhythmic chest compressions. "Come on, boyo. Come back to us!" she breathed while mentally counting each press on his sternum.

"Hey! You'll break his ribs. Be gentle with him!" yelled one of the boys.

Tamsin gauged her compression at five to six centimetres. An adequate depth to keep blood flowing to all the vital organs. "Trust me, I'm a nurse. This is no time for softness. I know it looks brutal and I might hurt his ribs but this is the only way to keep him going until the paramedics arrive."

"Okay, please don't let him die. He's my brother," said the girl tearfully.

"I'm doing my best. Boys, go to the road and bring the paramedics here, quickly. Girl, what's your name?" Tamsin asked continuing her compressions.

"We're on it," said the boy's dutifully running to find the ambulance.

"I'm Deanna, he's Rico,"

"Nice to meet you, Deanna. Drop down by his side. I need you to pinch his nose. Cup your mouth to his. Then give him a nice, deep breath of rescue air. Can you do that?"

Deanna nodded and followed the instructions.

Tamsin paused to allow Deanna's breath to inflate Rico's lungs, then began compressions again. For five minutes she and Deanna repeated the process until the paramedics arrived and took over.

The two male paramedics made quick work wiring the young footballer up to the defibrillator. They quickly mobilised their patient and rushed him to the resuscitation department.

Tamsin took a deep breath as the ambulance left. She found herself surrounded by the other two boys and Deanna.

"Will Rico be okay?" asked the boy who had run for help.

"There are no promises at this stage. The defibrillator did get his heart beating again which is great. For now, we must trust in the cardiologist to help him." Tamsin put her arms around Deanna. "You did well helping me save your brother."

"Thanks," she shook her head, "but you're a hero. I have to get to my mum and tell her what happened."

"Hmm, she'll panic!" Tamsin looked at her watch, she was already twenty minutes late for her interview. "Bugger it! Get in the car. I'll drive you home."

Almost an hour later, Tamsin returned to the hospital. Deanna and her mum were with her. With parting thanks, they rushed in to find Rico. "Well, here goes nothing," Tamsin sighed as she went to see if she could save her interview.

"Tamsin Wellesley – you're over an hour late. If a patient is waiting for surgery and you're late you could kill them. You understand that?" said Mr Whitely the chief surgeon at the hospital. The man who would become her employer if he accepted her. Right now, he looked set to strip her of her medical license instead of employing her.

"I know and am sorry, Mr Whitely. Ironically, I would have been fifteen minutes early, but I was flagged down by a boy. His footballer friend collapsed at the side of the University Park football pitch. Had I continued here to my interview instead of going to give him CPR, he'd be dead right now. I know as excuses go this is an extreme one, but if you call the emergency dispatch you can get them to check the logs. They will confirm I called the ambulance. My recommendation letter here proves I'm always punctual. I…"

"Thank you, Tamsin." Whitely took the letter from her. "Please, wait outside. Have a cup of coffee. I must interview another nurse, make some calls and deliberate before I can make my decision."

Tamsin looked at her shoes. "I understand. Thank you for not dismissing me on the spot."

"I won't keep you long." Whitely peered at her over his glasses as she left the office and closed the door behind her.

Tamsin felt her heart beat for every tick of the loud clock on the wall in the waiting room. Each tick seeming more ominous than the last. Every reason why she wouldn't get the job occurred to her in a continuous loop. Minutes into her anxiety-inducing wait the other prospective nurse came and entered the office for an interview. She left very soon after in tears.

Just as Tamsin imagined leaving the same way, Whitely appeared and beckoned her into the office. "Thank you for waiting, Tamsin," he said as he sat behind his spotless desk. "Young Rico Hernandez suffered a cardiac arrest as a result of a birth defect. He is undergoing corrective surgery as we speak and is expected to make a decent recovery."

"Oh, that's great news." Tamsin smiled. It was a wonderful feeling knowing she'd saved a precious life and knowing that young Rico would make it.

"He's getting that lifesaving surgery because you put your life, your future on hold. You knew being late for your interview would likely cost you your job and career. Regardless, you selflessly went down to that pitch and gave Rico CPR until the paramedics arrived." Whitely took off and began polishing his glasses, his eyes never wavering from the nurse sitting before him.

Tamsin felt uncomfortable beneath his gaze, her chest tightened leaving her dizzy. "I couldn't leave him to die. I had to help him, the kids didn't even have usable phones. I…"

"You did exactly what I would expect a nurse to do every single time a patient needs her. I checked out your recommendation letter and your credentials. From those, I have made a decision. The triage department can't have you back."

"But why?" Tamsin felt like she'd been shot. Why on earth would he make sure she couldn't have her old job if this one failed?

Whitely smiled. "I don't want them to have you. You Tamsin, are the perfect nurse to join my team. Your first shift starts at 8 a.m. on Monday."

"Unless somebody else requires CPR en route!"

"Quite right. Mind you, that's the only reason why you'll be allowed to be late." Whitely extended a hand.

Tamsin took a deep breath and shook it. "Thank you so much, Mr Whitely. I'll be here and ready." As she left the office, she gave a little fist pump. Saving a boy's life and getting her job had made this the best Friday of her life.

Lionized and Enchanted

Ralph Nestor was a young man on top of his game. He had A-list celebrity status, he'd starred in three number one films by top movie producers, and made an awful lot of money. Despite the fame and wealth, he wasn't happy. The constant buzz of paparazzi wherever he went and screaming fans all over the place was driving him nuts. How can a man live a happy life when he can't even take a piss in peace?

Fresh off filming a scene in his latest blockbuster, Ralph needed lunch. He headed into the city to seek out a quiet little place. Somewhere he might dine alone for once. He'd chosen denim jeans, a leather jacket, and dark glasses in the hope of remaining inconspicuous. However, that wasn't going to happen today.

"OMG! Look, girls. He's Ralph Nestor! Ooh, isn't he just the sexiest!" shrieked the woman coming out of a fashion store.

"Hmm, I'd love to get my hands on his cute little arse," said a blonde purring like an impassioned tiger.

"Get outta my way! I'm bedding him first!" cried another overcome by lust.

Ralph sighed as the air was filled with shrieks and screams. A hasty right turn took him through a rubbish-strewn alley. He dashed out the other side, and ducked into a little café. A glance through the window allowed him to breathe again; the women hadn't followed him – at least for now.

"Good afternoon, sir. Welcome to the Cocoa Bean Café. I have a nice table by the fireplace if you'd like to warm up."

Ralph turned to face the server. He felt her greeting very warm if a little odd as nobody was dining in the café just then. "Hello. That would be great, thank you," he said while

89

admiring her pretty navy pinafore dress and matching apron bearing the café's name. Smiling, he sat down at a teak table and glanced out the window. The coast was clear. "Nice little place you have here."

"Thank you, we're proud of it." The server presented him with the menu and gave him some time to peruse it. "What can I get you to eat and drink, sir?"

"Everything looks delicious. I think I'll have a BLT sandwich and a Café Americano to start please." Ralph handed back the menu, his eyes on a woman rushing past outside.

"I'll bring those right out to you, Sir. Let me know if you need anything else in the meantime," the server said watching another female dash by with a large camera in hand.

Ralph watched her walk around a teak-and-glass counter and step out the back. This was the first time in a while he felt he could relax with his lunch. The server returned and began making his coffee at the barista machine. It was then the café's door shot open and banged against the wall.

"I found him, girls! Let's see if he'll sign our T-shirts!" shrieked the woman from the fashion store earlier.

"There's that sex bomb! I'm getting him to sign my bra!" another called behind her as they barged in.

Ralph was about to stand when the server rushed past him.

"Ut-uh! No chance, ladies!" The server blocked their path and pointed to the door. "Nobody comes in this café to heckle and lionize my customers. You will leave now or I will have you arrested for breaching the peace."

"But he's Ralph—" the woman tried to dart around the server as camera flashes erupted through the window.

The server seized her by the shoulders and turned her

back toward the door. "I don't give a monkey's if he's Elvis Presley or the Pope – Get out!" This time the server forcibly injected the overexcited women. She locked the door and pulled the blinds on the windows, blocking the view of quite a crowd of camera-wielding people outside. "My apologies, Sir. Let me get your lunch for you, now."

"Thanks, I appreciate you doing that." Ralph relaxed again and was soon enjoying a good sandwich and coffee. The whole time the server was perfectly respectful and allowed him to dine in peace.

"Anything else I can get you?" she asked when he was done.

"Hmm, think I'll have a slice of lemon cheesecake, please. But, first, I'd like to know your name." Ralph turned his smoky-brown eyes on hers.

I server blushed under his gaze and retied her ponytail with shaking hands. "I'm Hannah. I'll go and get you that lemon cheesecake."

"There's no rush, Hannah. I wanted to thank you for the respect you're showing me. I know you recognised me from the moment I came in, didn't you?"

Hannah nodded. "I did. You came in for lunch like a normal customer and so that's how I treated you, that's all."

"Thank you for that. It's hard to find a place without cameras and screaming people all trying to lionize me all the time, these days." Ralph pulled out a seat and patted it. "Will you make that cheesecake for two and join me?"

Hannah blushed deeper. "I shouldn't."

Ralph reclined in his seat. "I thought you could take a little break seeing as you closed the café for me."

"Yeah, I suppose I did. Okay, thank you." Hannah was shaking as she fetched the cheesecakes and came to sit with the celebrity.

Seeing how nervous she was, Ralph gave a disarming

91

smile. "It's okay, please relax. I'm just a regular man with his face in too many places, that's all."

The remark made Hannah laugh at him.

"That's better. You have a beautiful smile, you know." Ralph savoured a slither of cheesecake. "Mmm, scrumptious."

"I'm glad you like it. Our baker makes it using my grandmother's old recipe." Hannah tried some and almost choked through her nervousness.

Ralph handed her a napkin. "Your grandmother must be very talented in the kitchen. Anyway, what does Hannah do when she's not treating her customers like kings and queens?"

"Thank you for the compliment."

"I'll be sure to repeat it on the café's review pages as well." Ralph beckoned her to answer his question.

"I'm boring. I write a few stories from time to time. I wanted to study to be a nurse. I got the grades at school but haven't enough money for the courses."

"Being a nurse is a very heroic job." Ralph forked another slice of cheesecake into his mouth and chewed thoughtfully. "Will you share some of your tales with me?"

Hannah looked shocked at the request. "Oh, they're pretty ordinary. You don't want to read them."

Hearing her talk that way upset Ralph a little bit. "Hey! There are enough people in this world who will criticise and demean you and your work. You don't need to beat yourself up as well. Please, try to be confident in your abilities for me, hey?"

"I will, I'm sorry."

"It's okay. Look, why do you write your stories?"

"Well..." Hannah stared into the remains of her cheesecake. "I love my characters and writing about them, that's all."

"Then your stories will be beautiful. Tell you what. Do you know Ristorante Italiano on St Clement Street?"

"Yes, it's really expensive."

"That's the one. When you finish work, go and fetch your stories and meet me there for dinner at seven tonight. Then I can meet your characters and enjoy them too."

"But, I – why are you spending your time on me. I'm just a lowly waitress."

"No buts. You're a special, talented, respectful person. You gave me a wonderful lunch in peace. I'd like to get to know you better and maybe help you as a reward. For now, I have to get back to the set and finish my recordings for the day. I look forward to seeing you this evening." Ralph stood and handed her some money for his lunch – adding a large tip. "To start with, put the extra in your college fund."

"Thank you, sir." Hannah went red again. "Come out the back so you don't get mauled!" She led him through and unlocked the door for him.

Ralph returned to work deep in thought. By the time he met Hannah at the restaurant, he'd contacted the local university and paid for her nursing courses in full. He wasn't sure what to expect with her stories. However, if they were good he would ensure Hollywood producers and publishers saw them very soon.

Mitzi's Miracle

Even with the harsh, dry, and cold air biting at her reddened cheeks, Mitzi smiled at the falling snow.

The cruel wind whipped about her hair as she looked about the spruce and pine trees carpeting the snow-covered hills. She was standing in a festive wilderness perfect for cards and puzzles, she decided.

Mitzi gazed back the way she came and let out a sigh of relief at seeing no lanterns following on behind her. She knew being caught doing something this flippant would land her in serious trouble. There was no doubt punishment for this would seriously deplete her Christmas present pile, maybe for several years.

Still – a girl had to follow her heart – didn't she?

With a deep, steamy breath, she trudged through the frozen air. She loved how her lantern turned the layer of fluffy ice golden before her. Mitzi hauled her brown leather boot out of a two foot deep snow drift and adjusted her red satchel. She thought her boots were too posh especially when considering the extortionate price, but her daddy had insisted. At least they were warm and looked nice with her heavy red dress today.

Soon she came upon a little log cabin. The sight of a thin column of smoke and a glow at the window drew a fresh smile to her near-frozen face. Mitzi knew this was her daddy's summer hunting cabin. This winter it was still in use for a special reason.

Through snowdrifts and a curtain of sparkling flakes, Mitzi arrived at the door and knocked with her gloved hand.

A chair scraped across the floor and something thumped as if thrown into a bin. Then the door opened revealing a teenage boy. With ragged trousers and a holed jumper, it was clear he'd fallen on hard times. "Mitzi! Why did you come out

94

here on such a treacherous night? Why, you could wind up with your arm in a sling and your leg in a cast in this snow!"

"Good evening to you too, Jonah. Mitzi reached out and hugged him. "Are you okay?"

Jonah nodded, took her hand and led her inside so he could shut the door on the cold. "Thanks to you and this cabin I'm doing just fine."

"That's great." Mitzi gazed around the cabin. It had a simple wooden kitchen with a log burner for warmth and cooking. A single bed and a couple of old chairs and a beaten up table made up the rest of the furniture. She shuddered as her eyes met those of the stuffed moose head with its enormous antlers, mounted above the bed; she hated that thing. "I brought you more food," she said handing him her satchel.

"You shouldn't have taken such a risk." Jonah helped her sit in a chair and knelt before her.

"I got you here to save your life. I'm not going to let you freeze and starve, now." Mitzi remembered one night a month ago. Jonah lived in the same wealthy street as she did. He'd been working at a posh restaurant and was fired for giving food to the homeless without permission. Within hours his father had also cast him out, saying he couldn't live at home without paying rent. In the cold of winter, Jonah became a penniless vagabond all for the sake of being charitable. Mitzi's daddy forbade her from getting involved. She couldn't and wouldn't leave her neighbour to die when she could help. Every night she could since, she supplied him with food, blankets, and other essentials.

"I'm more grateful than you know." Jonah smiled as he unbuckled her boots and began to remove them. "Your feet must be frozen."

"Just a bit," Mitzi blushed at the sensation of him kissing her toes.

The boy massaged her cold feet for a few moments before rising to add logs to the burner. Returning to her, he wrapped a blanket about her shoulders.

"Thank you. I see you put the axe to good use." Mitzi indicated the log splitting tool she'd smuggled to the cabin for him.

"Being able to chop fuel for this fire is saving my life." Jonah took the satchel to the kitchen work surface. He took out a couple of tins of beans and soup, a loaf of bread, margarine, and jam, and a fruit cake. There was something else that brought tears to his eyes. "What's this?" he asked revealing a little box wrapped in rich red and gold paper.

"I probably won't be able to escape for a few days over Christmas. I wanted to bring your gift today instead." Mitzi smiled coyly. "Go on, open it early."

Jonah's eyes sparkled as he tore into the paper. He revealed a velvet jewellery box. Inside that was a brown leather and bead bracelet. It had a silver tree pendant glittering on one side. "I love it. Thank you, sweet Mitzi."

"The tree is the symbol of the Ent – the guardians of the forest. They say if you wear this, the Ent will always protect you." Mitzi explained.

Jonah put the bracelet on and admired it. "I feel safer already. I don't deserve it."

"Sure, you do. Remember all this bad stuff happened because you are a nice charitable person. Something the wealthy snobs we call parents can never understand."

Jonah wiped his eyes and turned away from her. "I don't have parents anymore. From now on, I must find my own way to live on this greed-ridden planet."

"Yes, and you will do yourself proud – I know it." Mitzi rose to her feet. She unbuttoned her white fur coat and dropped it on the chair. "Do you remember what you asked to do with me last night?"

"I do. I wanted to take you to the Christmas ball and then dance the night away with you."

"While we can't do that…" Mitzi wove her fingers into his. "Will you dance with me now?"

Jonah turned and gasped as he took in her beautiful, festive, evening dress. "You should be dancing with a prince – not this sorry old pauper."

"I don't want to spend my life with a stuck-up old nutcracker." Mitzi began to turn with him. "Having money means nothing if you can't enjoy sharing with those in need."

"Well, you're making me feel rich this evening," Jonah felt his nose brush hers as their lips met in a kiss warmer than the chilly cabin. As they continued to turn in each other's arms he left his forehead against hers. "I have something to tell you."

"Go ahead. Mitzi gulped, she just knew she wouldn't like what he said next.

"I won't be here tomorrow night. I…"

"Why? Where will you go? You can't survive out there."

"I don't think I'll be alive here much longer either. Your parents must be growing suspicious by now. I have to leave and go somewhere else before they catch us together."

"No, please don't. I'm not being followed." Mitzi felt herself shaking.

"You will be. Mitzi, I have to go."

"No, you don't. We…" Warm tears splashed onto her cheeks.

"I won't allow them to punish you for helping me." Jonah gently wiped her tears with his fingers. Smoothing her pretty hair he added, "I love you and that's the reason I have to go."

"I love—"

The cabin door crashed open. A man wearing a thick leather and fur coat turned white with snow, stalked in.

"Father, please!"

"Mitzi! I forbade you from helping this sorry excuse for a man. I…"

"Don't blame her, Mr Dorrance. I—"

"Shut your mouth, thief!"

"No, Father. He's a good person. His only crime was helping people who'd fallen on tough times. He wasn't committing theft – he was committing charity. He—"

"Enough! While I don't blame you for falling for this criminal's charms – you will be punished severely." Dorrance seized Jonah by the jumper and cracked his jaw with a savage punch.

The boy staggered and fell over a chair. Landing by the stove, he climbed drunkenly to his feet.

Dorrance made to strike him again but Mitzi blocked him.

"Stop it, Father! He's suffered enough already without you hurting – Argh!" Mitzi shrieked as her cheek burned from a withering slap.

Dorrance seized her shoulders and threw her onto the bed. "Stupid girl! Get your coat and boots on now!"

By then Jonah was seething. "How dare you hit her!" he yelled while balling his fists. "You have a beautiful, kind-hearted and charitable daughter. Instead of being proud of her, you abuse—"

Dorrance swung for him.

Jonah blocked and landed a punch of his own.

Dorrance's heavy coat spared him pain. "She's my daughter. I'll treat her how I like!" he screamed as he drove the boy into the cabin wall.

Pinned again by his jumper, Jonas thrust his head forward catching the rich man's chin with a sickening head-butt. Breaking free, he spun away toward the bed. "You should learn to act with your heart, instead of your wallet.

Maybe then, you could see the pain and suffering you inflict just like my father did!"

"I'll kill you, for that!" Dorrance drew a revolver from inside his coat.

"No, Father!" Mitzi screamed.

"Mitzi run!" Jonah demanded.

"Try to steal my daughter from me!" Dorrance pulled back the hammer and aimed.

"Please, Father. I love you. He is not taking me away; I'm just looking after…

"He is a filthy thieving vagabond. A homeless vagrant. The Duchy's son, William, will want nothing to do with you if he sees you with him!"

"Good! I don't want nothing to do with him anyway." Mitzi glared at her daddy while pulling on her coat.

"Foolish, girl." Dorrance saw Jonah move and tracked him with the gun. "William's going to make you very rich. Whether you like it or not, you will marry—"

"Like hell, I will. You blame Jonah for trying to steal me away. The only reason I'm going right now is because of you!" Mitzi yelled through furious sobs.

"Mitzi, please – just go – now!" Jonah demanded.

"He's right, daughter. Go, you don't want to see what happens when I shoot him!" Dorrance almost smiled at the murderous thought.

"Father, you're insane." Mitzi took Jonah's hand. "Come on, let's go together."

"I…" Jonah leapt at Dorrance but he was too late.

The solid blam of a gunshot erupted through the tension in the room.

Mitzi screamed, convulsed and dropped like a stone.

Jonah slammed into Dorrance and drove him to the floor.

A second gunshot rang out.

Dorrance climbed to his feet and cried out in horror.

Both Mitzi and Jonah lay dead.

For the longest time, Dorrance cradled his lifeless daughter's body in his arms. Through floods of tears, he realised charity and love were more important than money. Only now it was all too late.

Sometime after midnight, he dragged the bodies outside and covered them with snow. He would return in spring and bury them properly then.

Hours later a grey and white husky dog came to a stop behind the cabin. He looked back and sniffed his paw prints in the snow. He lifted his majestic head to the sky, he howled.

"What is it, Blizzard?" asked a man striding over wearing thick black boots. His voice was gravelly with an age matching his long white beard and curly hair. Noticing the bump in the snow he nodded. "Oh, I see we were too late."

Blizzard whimpered.

"Well, we can't have that now, can we?" said the old man having a nip of whisky from his old flask. "Yo!"

Blizzard gave an excited bark and began to dig. Within minutes Mitzi and Jonah's bodies lay uncovered. They were frozen stiff and blue. Yet they seemed to be looking at each other with love even in death.

"Well done, Blizzard. Now it's my turn." The old man took a simple brown pouch from his pocket. Taking some red and gold shimmering dust from within, he sprinkled it liberally over the two bodies.

Blizzard barked his approval.

The bodies were soon surrounded by a pool of steaming warm water. They turned pink with warmth and life.

Mitzi coughed as she opened her eyes, then sat up.

Beside her, Jonah did the same.

They hugged as if seeing each other for the first time in years.

The old man stood back with Blizzard and smiled as Mitzi set eyes on him.

"My father killed us both. I don't know how you did it, but I know we must thank you for our lives," she managed.

"Dear, Mitzi, Master Jonah, when people give the gift of kindness, there are always those who take note. Especially those searching for employees."

"Pardon me," Jonah said rising with Mitzi cuddled in his arms.

"Jonah, it began with you. Molly Starlight, my snow-globe gazer witnessed you helping the homeless. She was distraught when you were fired and then made homeless for your charity."

"I still don't regret helping those poor homeless people. Especially the children," Jonah said.

"Oh, I know. Mitzi. Molly continued to watch Jonas' plight. She was delighted when you put your kind and caring heart on show. She loved how you risked everything to help Jonah survive the winter."

"I couldn't let him freeze and starve to death when all he did was help people." Mitzi wiped her eyes. "Then my dad killed me."

"Indeed. He'll be getting no presents for the rest of his life, I assure you." The old man winked. "Anyway, would you like some charitable jobs?"

"What sort of jobs?" Mitzi said feeling suspicious of the old magical man.

"Only the most kind-hearted people get to work for me. Mitzi, you will become my manager of merriment. Spreading happiness around the world. Jonah, you will become my manager of festive jokes. The last joke elf ran out of laughter last summer you see."

Mitzi looked to Jonah and the two nodded. Their old lives were gone. Time to start new ones. "We accept," she said.

"Yo!" cheered the old man glowing with happiness. As fresh snow began falling, he tapped his foot, filling the air with gold sparkles. At that moment, he, Blizzard, Mitzi and Jonah disappeared. After all, there was just a few days left to get everything ready for the big day in Lapland!

Passage of Kindness

Come rain or shine, wind or snow – out for a walk with the dog you must go.

The little rhyme echoed in Emma's mind as she walked. Her grandmother had told her that when she got her first dog at the age of five. She stuck to it too; she'd had several dogs and walked them all every single day regardless of the weather.

That's why she was in the park this dreary autumnal day. She strolled along beneath her pink umbrella with Wilson the miniature schnauzer at her feet.

There were few people about today, something that pleased her as a quiet park was a peaceful place to walk. The rains kept the birds out of sight too. Except for the enormous flock of feral pigeons congregating around the pond anyway. Emma was aware the city council had held a meeting. They'd voted to cull the pigeons to reduce the damage they caused to the park and surrounding buildings.

Wilson growled at a pair of pigeons who strayed too close.

"Hey, Willy. Shush! Those pigeons have enough problems with the council without you barking at them." Emma walked on feeling relaxed by the pitter-patter of rain upon her umbrella.

Emma made a right turn and walked between an avenue of trees whose leaves were turning from vivid red to magnificent gold and earthy brown as they prepared for winter.

On a bench, in the shelter of a thick pine tree, was old Joe. He was a homeless man who'd lived in and around the park for as long as Emma could remember. As always, he was wearing the same old filthy trousers and shirt beneath his old wax jacket. His weathered features were half-hidden behind his bristling beard.

Today he was listening to the weather on his beaten-up portable radio. "Good afternoon, Miss Emma," he said with a cheery wave of his dirty hand.

"Hello, Joe." Emma smiled and approached him. "How are you?"

"Managing as always."

Wilson gave a friendly bark and pressed his front paws against the old man's leg with a cheery wag of his tail.

"Hi, Wilson. Looking after Emma, are you?" Joe scratched his chin.

"He's my little guardian angel." Emma glanced about the man's possessions on the bench and at his feet. There was no sign of food packets or bottles of water anywhere. She could almost guarantee he hadn't consumed anything today. "Here, go and get something to eat and drink," she said handing him a twenty-pound note.

"Thank you kindly, Miss Emma. I feel bad, keep taking money from you," Joe said through teary eyes.

"Well, don't. I earn way more than Willy and I need to live comfortably. It's a pleasure to help you out a little bit as well." Emma bent and ignored his unwashed smell as she hugged him. "Now, go on and have a nice meal."

"I will. Thanks again, Miss Emma." Old Joe tipped an imaginary hat and rose to his feet to gather his meagre possessions. "Thank you too, Wilson. Wishing you a wonderful evening."

"Have a good evening, Joe." Emma grinned to herself as she strode away along the rain-soaked paths. She always felt a warmth in her heart knowing she'd given the old man a little help and a smile.

Emma continued along the pavement lost in thought about how she might help Joe find a retirement home to live in or something.

Wilson barked and strained at the lead.

Emma flinched, following the dog's direction. She saw a red helium balloon floating beneath the canopy of trees. "Wilson! You, silly dog. It's only a balloon!" she chastised.

Wilson barked again, letting a growl deepen his doggy voice.

This time, Emma realised she wasn't alone. A young man wearing a long, dark coat, jeans and black shirt had walked up close behind her. "Hello," she said increasing her pace.

"Hi, darlin'. You're setting the park ablaze with your beauty this afternoon."

Emma sighed. Chat-up lines from pompous gits like him had the same effect as sleeping pills on her. "I'm not interested. Please leave me alone."

Wilson, sensing his mistress's energy and disliking the man, backed up her words with a murderous growl.

"Ahh, come on, darlin'. Look at you. Prancing along wearing that little black, lacy dress all split to the hip. Course you're interested."

"I'd rather make love to a hog than show interest in a sleazy git like you!" Emma shot him a glare as she ushered Wilson along the path. Her heart was pounding in her chest but she controlled her fears by igniting her ire. "And, for your information the way a lady dresses has no bearing on her desires. Now, go away!"

The man kept pace with her. He sniffed the air loudly. "I smell lies and the most beautiful perfume."

Emma shook her head. She chose not to dignify him with a response and just kept walking.

"By your beautiful body and curvaceous bum, I bet you're a steak salad girl. I know the perfect restaurant. It has a hotel just ready for some bedroom Olympics upstairs too if you get my meaning."

Emma hid a smile; she was vegetarian so he was half

right. "I'm not going anywhere with you. If you touch me, you'll be spending the night in the hospital getting your testicles reattached!"

"Ooh, fiery! I love that in a woman. Getting hot and horny now, aren't—" The man reached beneath her umbrella and groped her shoulder.

Wilson lunged for his leg, sinking his teeth into the man's jeans.

Emma noticed a sweaty smell mixing with the petrichor. She pulled Wilson away and turned in time to see Joe wrench the man away from her.

The homeless man pulled back his right hand and punched the creep square on the nose. With a handful of coat, he sent him sprawling along the wet path. "The lady told you to leave her alone. If I see you within fifty feet of her or any other lady again, I'll kill you. Now get lost!" he yelled with gusto.

The man picked himself up and sprinted along the path, disappearing towards an exit from the park.

"Hi, Joe. Thank you so much for getting rid of him," Emma said with a grateful smile despite the fear still fuelling her with adrenaline.

Wilson made a fuss of the old man.

"I saw him cut across the grass to catch you. That was all I needed to know that he was up to no good." Joe collected his bags from beneath a tree and returned a smile, full of missing and yellow teeth. "At least now I've repaid you for some of the money you've given me over the years."

Emma wiped her eyes as she realised the danger she'd been in. "You did more than that. I think you just saved my life."

"Maybe so. Who knows what horrors like him are capable of? At least he's gone now." Joe began walking alongside Emma. "Would you like me to walk you home?"

"You're a sweetheart, Joe. It's hard to fathom how such a

lovely gentleman could end up living in the park," Emma said.

"Well, it's a long story. I had a beautiful wife and a daughter when I was your age," Joe said. "That was a good time of life. I had a good job – everything a man could want to be happy. Then we went on holiday to Majorca. The sun, sand and sea were wonderful. Our plane crashed on the way home. My wife and daughter died, but I survived. Every day I wonder why the fates chose to save me instead of my precious girls."

Emma couldn't stop tears flowing down her face. "Aww, Joe. That's awful, I'm so sorry."

"Thank you. Anyway, I'd had my heart ripped right out of my chest. I couldn't focus or function on anything anymore. I lost my job and then my home and that's when I came to live in the park. I have loads of friends in the wildlife now."

"While I'm pleased the wildlife keep you company. I want you to know you didn't deserve any of that. You're a lovely man." Emma tightened Wilson's leash as they reached the road. "I think the fates spared you because you have lots of love to give. Like you did to me when you saved me from that creep.

"Maybe so." Joe strolled along with his arms behind his back. "You remember falling into the park pond when you were maybe four years old?"

Emma shook her head as they crossed the road through the light traffic. "I—" She paused as the memory returned. An icy splash. Her mum screaming and then "I remember. You saved me, didn't you?"

"I did. I jumped right in and returned you to your mother. I near froze my bum off that night in my wet clothes. However, I proudly watched you growing up every day since then.

"Aww, that's sweet. Thank you, Joe."

They'd arrived at the City Hotel.

107

Emma opened the door and stepped inside, beckoning Joe in behind her.

"Oh, do you live here?" Joe asked looking confused.

"No." Emma approached the counter.

"Hi, I'm sorry there are no dogs allowed in the hotel," said the receptionist behind the rich cedar counter.

"That's okay, he's not staying. I'd like to pay for a single room with breakfast for a week please." Emma said.

"Certainly." The receptionist spent a few moments doing all the computer work for the booking and assigned a key card. She took payment and handed over the key and receipt. "Enjoy your stay."

"Thank you." Emma smiled and turned to Joe. "There you are, room seven is all yours for the next seven days. You'll have breakfast waiting each morning too."

"I can't—" Joe began, his bottom lip trembling.

"You saved my life, Joe. Please, enjoy your room as my thank you." Emma pressed the key into his hand.

"You're a wonderful lady, Miss Emma. Thank you." Joe was beaming from ear to ear as he walked up the steps to find his room.

Emma returned home with Wilson. Joe's sad story resonated in her mind as she enjoyed a cup of coffee. She made up her mind then, by the time he left the hotel she'd have somewhere permanent for him to stay.

On day six of Joe's stay at the hotel, she handed him the keys to a little caretaker's cottage. The place was his rent-free; all he had to do was take care of the grounds of the manor house it resided upon. It even afforded him a little wage to look after himself on.

Emma had changed his life. With a little love and care we can all help those around us and be happy as a result.

Patience of a Saint

"Hey, Gaston. Can you come here, please?" waitress Avril called whilst polishing tables within the Ristorante Gallo. This was her third week working here and she was loving it.

Gaston was the chef-owner. He came through humming an Italian classic. "What can I help you with, Avril?" he asked in his always cheerful voice.

"Look outside the front door. That beagle's been there since I arrived an hour go. Wonder what he wants?"

From inside was just possible to see the top of the beagle's soft brown head and hopeful eyes. The rest of him was hidden by the green woodwork of the restaurant's façade.

"How funny! He was probably in the alley when the butcher came this morning. He's hoping you'll offer him a steak, I'd bet." Gaston chuckled and repositioned his tall chef's hat.

"I don't think that's it. Go closer," Avril urged. The young waitress walked behind the bar to put her cleaning things away.

"Very, well." Gaston walked to the front door.

The beagle popped up on his back legs and pawed the glass with a whimper. Beside him, a biscuit lay uneaten.

"You see. His pads are scratched up. I think he's been running for a long distance. Also, he wasn't interested in the food I gave him."

"I see…" Gaston opened the door and knelt.

The beagle whimpered as he threw himself on the chef in a flurry of paws and fur.

"I know this dog. This is Claude; his mistress comes here every so often." Gaston steadied the dog and began to gently stroke his soft fur and comfort him. "What are you doing here, boy? Where's Amelie?"

"You think she's in trouble?" Avril suggested while smiling at the antics of the dog. He was now pulling on the chef's sleeve as if trying to get him out of the restaurant.

"I don't know. Whatever the case we have to go and find out." Gaston stood up. Can you get him some water while I change?"

"Sure. Come here, Claude." Avril beckoned.

The beagle gave a little bark and returned to sitting outside.

"Fine, you stay out there then." Avril smiled and brought the water to him instead.

Claude had a couple of licks. He was too stressed and desperate to have more.

Gaston returned swiftly. "I've locked the back doors. Will you come with me in case I need help?"

"Of course." Avril pulled on her coat and followed him out as he locked the restaurant.

Gaston and Avril put the beagle in his Citroen and set off through the narrow streets of Paris. "We'll try Amelie's home first."

"Just as well you know where she lives," Avril said smoothing the dog's ears trying to keep him calm. Passing the Eifel tower should be a treat but not when you'd seen it every day of your life. Avril barely glanced at it as she focused on the dog.

"Amelie was taken ill last year. For a while, I prepared my delicious soups and personally delivered them to her."

"Aww, Gaston. That's so sweet of you to do that for her." Avril hugged Claude. "Isn't he a sweetie? Hey, boy?"

Claude gave a little bark.

"See! Even he agrees."

Gaston's cheeks turned a deep shade of pink. "Well, it's nice to help where you can." The chef indicated into a street lined with Belle Epoque terraced houses. He pulled up behind a small van and glanced at house number six. "Let's see what's going on."

Avril opened her door to get out.

Claude leapt into the road, barked, and set off along the street.

"Oh, no! Claude! I'm sorry, Gaston!" Avril cried as she ran after him.

Claude shot through the legs of a lady of flamboyant style with her gaudy dress and haircut.

"We're sorry!" Avril said as she dashed by turning the lady in a circle.

"Not your fault. I think Claude's leading the way. Come on!" Gaston caught Avril and the two ran flat out to keep up with the dog. "He's got plenty of energy despite his sore paws!"

"No kidding!"

The beagle outpaced both of them as he swung between parked cars.

"Claude, no!" Gaston yelled.

Horns blared as little dog crossed the street right in front of braking cars. Tyres screeched and people swore. Claude reached the pavement unscathed and stopped by the door to an old chapel.

"Phew, he made it!" Avril gulped for air as they caught up. "Looks like he wants us in there."

Claude barked and pawed at the ancient oak door.

"Amelie told me about this place. This is the Chapel of St Jacques." Gaston pointed to the historic monument sign on a nearby post. "It's been closed to the public for about a decade. Amelie was helping to raise funds to get it renovated and reopened after it became unsafe."

"Okay, so why would she be in there now?"

"That, Avril, is a very good question." Gascon tried the door and found it open.

111

Claude immediately bounded inside.

"Come on," Gaston beckoned as he stepped inside.

"Go slowly. Be careful!" Avril urged. She retrieved her phone for a torch and followed him inside. Her light played off the billowing dust motes floating all around the building like lost spirits.

It seemed like an ordinary little chapel on the outside. Inside it opened into a lost treasure. An aisle bordered by beautifully carved pews ran to a circular altar surrounded by formally beautiful stained-glass windows filled with religious scenes. A beam of sunlight cut through a hole in the roof and fell upon the altar stone. The effect was as if God was taking a sermon.

"Amelie! Are you in here?" Gaston yelled.

"Look at this poor place," Avril said saddened by the heaps of dust and debris from falling ceiling and broken windows. Even the floor had collapsed in one place. "Such a shame this beautiful chapel fell into ruin like this."

"It's a travesty. That's why Amelie was trying to rescue – Amelie!" Gaston sprinted between the pews and ran to the left of the altar.

Avril followed. There was Amelie. Half-buried in collapsed roof trusses and debris. Claude was sitting by her, licking her wrinkled face. Avril wiped away tears as she called the emergency services for the old lady.

"Amelie, it's going to be okay. Claude bought us to you. We'll save you now," Gaston said beginning to dig her out of the rubble.

The noise and Claude's licking brought her back from unconsciousness. "Gaston? Oh, Gaston."

"Yes, it's me, Amelie. Take it easy, you're going to be okay." The chef knelt and kissed her forehead. "You were so silly coming in here alone."

"I've always been a stupid old fool!" Amelie said

disdainfully. "My family are all buried in the crypt beyond this fallen roof. Coming here every day is the only way I can be with them. To not feel alone for a while."

"An ambulance is on its way," Avril said. "Amelie, this is the first time we've met. But I want you to know, you never have to be alone. Gaston and I will always be at the restaurant and a phone call away. We're here for you."

"Yes we are, you just have to ask. We promise to do something about this place too," said Gaston hugging her and the dog carefully.

Almost a year later Amelie stood on crutches in the chapel with Claude at her feet. Gaston and Avril stood on either side of her. Over the last eleven months, the chef and waitress had put together numerous charity events from the restaurant. Between them, they raised enough to fix the chapel. Now a new priest had been ordained as curator to the beautifully restored building.

"Welcome one and all to the Chapel of St Jacques and Saint Claude. Saint Claude is no ordinary Saint. He is a living and breathing beagle. Through heroically running through Paris to find his friend chef Gaston, he saved his mistress Amelie from an awful death. He also saved this beautiful building by bringing it to the attention of chef Gaston and waitress Avril. Over the last year, they selflessly worked to save our beautiful chapel whilst being friends to all those who require one. That's why we ordain this beagle "Saint Claude" and bless you both Gaston and Avril!"

Serendipity Mews

A flash of green in the ditch; a colour so unnatural in the dead of winter. Indy saw it again in the rear-view mirror. A car was definitely in the ditch. It wasn't surprising really, what with the sharp frost and foggy conditions this morning.

"This is going to make me late for work!" Indy grumbled. She was a clerk at an architect's office. Not a bad job for an eighteen-year-old, but boy was it boring! She pulled over, flicked the hazard lights on and climbed from the car. Pulling on a Hi-Viz vest and boots she kept in the boot, she headed back along the road to the stricken vehicle.

Almost on its side in the ditch was an estate car with darkened rear windows. Its engine was still running and the windscreen was shattered. Gouges in the earth showed it had travelled a fair way along the field drainage system before becoming stuck.

Indy climbed down and peered through the windows. There was a man slumped in the driving seat and cages in the back. That was enough for Indy to make a call to emergency services. With them on the way she levered the passenger's door open. At once the unmistakable smell of cats assailed her nostrils. She could hear mewing in the back too. "Good morning, lovely. You chose a bad place to park but don't worry; help's on the way." Indy could see the airbag had caused bruising to his face and maybe a broken nose. His arms were a mass of bleeding glass cuts from the shattered windows. There was no telling what other injuries he'd suffered. She knew he'd have to stay where he was until help arrived. If she tried to free him, she'd injure him further maybe fatally.

At her touch the driver roused. "Tha-nk yo-u. Sa-ve the cats," he managed before passing out again.

114

Signs Indy was sure of internal injuries. She reached over him and turned the ignition off. "Hang in there, okay. Everything's gonna be fine." Looking over the seats she was amazed to see the back was almost full of cages, each containing at least one cat or kitten. "Hey, kitties, I'll make sure you're all okay too. I promise." Despite a lump in her throat, Indy smiled; she always had a preference for cats over dogs. Was this serendipity then, that she'd come across the crashed car? She didn't know but was going to do all she could do help its occupants.

She took the keys, extracted herself from the car and clambered around the back. With some difficulty she managed to unlock and force the boot lid open. By the time the police, paramedics and a fire engine arrived, she'd lined-up fifteen cages on the verge and counted eleven adult cats and fourteen kittens of various ages. All of them seemed neglected and filthy. Some had minor injuries from the crash but mercifully they were all doing reasonably well.

"Morning. Were they all in the car?" asked a police officer.

"Yes, I couldn't get the driver out. I promised to look after his kitties and so I've gotten them out to safety." Indy frowned. "I don't know what I should do with them now, though."

The officer tickled a kitten through the cage. "Neither do I. It'll do no good taking them back to the police station. We don't have handcuffs or cells small enough."

Indy grinned at the joke. Her smile vanished quickly as the stress of the situation took over. It was miraculous watching the rescue team cutting part of the car away and freeing the driver. Within ten minutes, he was out of the car and in the back of the ambulance receiving treatment. Then with him on his way to the hospital, everybody began to leave the scene.

"Good luck with the cats," said the officer with a cheery wave before he drove away.

With him gone, Indy was alone with the twenty-five cats, a wrecked car, and a couple of crash scene investigators.

"You should go, love," called one of the men photographing the ditch.

"I would if I could. But I can't leave the cats here. The RSPCA told me they can't send anybody; they're too busy." Indy wiped her eyes. "That means if I go, these poor kitties die here at the side of the road. I won't let that happen!"

The investigator shook his head. "That's a terrible situation. There must be something that—"

Indy stormed past him back to the wrecked car. The fire brigade had cut the roof and most of the driver side panels away to extract the driver. She leaned inside and began searching for clues.

"Love, you can't be in there. You might be contaminating evidence," remarked the investigator putting on a hand on her shoulder.

"My name's Indy – not love! And this was a crash, not a murder. There has to be something in this car to do with the cats. Something, that'll tell me where he was taking them." Indy gave him a pleading look. "If I can find that, the cats have a chance. Don't you see?"

The investigator smiled and nodded. "That's the way, lo-Indy. We didn't see you breaking the law," he told her with a wink.

"Thank you." Indy returned her focus to the car. A poke around revealed a sheaf of papers in the passenger's footwell. "So, you're Adam Clements and you're taking the cats to the Four Paws sanctuary which—" Indy gasped. This was a court authorised seizure notice for the cats. Adam owned the sanctuary and had rescued the cats from a

116

hoarder house only for them to need rescuing again. It was so terrible it left her close to tears.

With an address in hand, Indy's resolve to help the cats and Adam tightened. She flattened the seats in her car and loaded all the cats inside. She was forced to transfer a couple of the cats into occupied cages to make them fit but she was able to drive away with all twenty-five cats.

Thirty minutes later, Indy arrived at the sanctuary with her new feline friends.

A concerned looking lady was bottle feeding a puppy at the gate. "I'm sorry, we're closed today."

"Hi, my name's Indy. My car's full of cats. Adam Clements was bringing them here. I'm afraid he had a car crash on the way."

"Oh, no! I knew something bad happened!" The lady almost dropped the puppy as grief set in.

"It'll be okay. Adam's in hospital by now and getting treatment. I'm hopeful, he'll recover in time." Indy hugged her. "Can I bring the cats inside?"

"Oh – I er yes please do. I'm Tanya. Adam's my husband. We run the sanctuary alone. I can't be with him and look after the cats at the same time. Ooh, I don't know what to do!"

Indy opened her mouth to speak. Her phone rang instead. She instinctively knew it was her boss wondering where she was, and so answered it. "Yes, Paul. I came upon a car crash. I'm trying to rescue some cats that were—"

"Cats! Bugger the cats, I need you at work!"

Indy felt her ire rising as she looked at Tanya still fretting with her puppy. "I won't be coming in at least this morning – maybe at all today. I'm sorry, Paul."

"Then you'll fail your deadline. I can't allow that."

"Some things are more important than work, Paul. I'll catch up tomorrow."

"No, you either get in within the next thirty minutes or you're fired!" Paul bellowed down the phone.

"Fine! I quit!" Indy hung-up and pocketed her phone with a smile at Tanya. "Need an assistant?"

"I can't believe you just did that!" Tanya looked stunned.

"Neither can I! I should have done that weeks ago." Indy chuckled. "Right, show me where the cats go and I'll take care of them. You get to Adam's side and I'll be here until you get back," she instructed.

Tanya hugged her again. "You're wonderful. Thank you."

Indy was soon in full swing at the sanctuary. She had a vet check the cats as she got them comfortable in cages. The other fifteen dogs, cats, rabbits and the llama, she ensured were fed and happy. She saw to the dog's needs and spent the day enjoying herself with the animals. By the time Tanya returned that evening, Indy was tired but happy. "How's, Adam?" she asked.

"He's awake following surgery to remove his spleen. He'll be fine in a few days, they reckon." Tanya looked at all the new arrivals and checked her sanctuary. "Name tags filled in, cats all clean, fed and watered. Fresh litter in all cages. You've done us proud in here."

"I walked all the dogs this afternoon too. Everybody should be happy until tomorrow." Indy replied. "I'm glad Adam's going to be alright."

"Thank you, Indy. It seems the only one not alright is you. I mean, you haven't got a job because you were a kind and wonderful young lady helping us today." Tanya led the way to her kitchen and prepared tea, soup and rolls for them both. "I won't stand for it, you know," she said while stirring her soup.

"What?" Indy asked sitting at the table with her tea.

"You losing your job like that. Neither will Adam. I told him what happened. He and I have been planning to hire a sanctuary assistant and manager for a while. We'd love that person to be you." Tanya put a bowl before Indy and smiled. "What do you think?"

"It's been a day of kitties and serendipity which led to you offering me an unexpected job." Indy sighed as she enjoyed the rich vegetable soup. "You know what, my preference was never to work in a boring office anyway. I accept and thank you so much!"

The Biggest Secret

Since Alicia and I moved in together, things haven't exactly gone well. The worst of the issues is money. We scrimped and saved to make it work. Our bed was nothing but a mattress propped on pallets. We lived in a tiny one-bedroom apartment with the smallest kitchen you've ever seen. Every sacrifice was worthwhile for the love we shared.

We grew close at university. Although we'd flit between lovers, we'd always come back to each other. We were smitten and the growing fervour between us only proved that. Lately, we'd both found work and things were beginning to improve.

Alicia was out of bed before me. She returned with a pot of freshly ground coffee. The Italian blend was rich and strong, just what a man needed to start the day.

We sat on the bed to drink. She smoothed my long mousey hair and kissed my cheek.

"Dear, Alicia. It pleases the butterflies in my heart to see you bright and bubbly this morning," I said with my hands clasped about my mug.

Alicia just smiled.

"Kissing me in such a tender way can only mean you still love me. Which means my morning has begun most wonderfully."

She leaned in close and whispered, "I have a secret to tell you, Gino."

I felt a wave of trepidation fluttering through me like a chill. It was not one of fear but of anticipation. "My ears are yours, darling."

Alicia sipped her coffee and shook her head. Teasing me with that glint in her eyes and cheekiness in her smile. "Ut-ha, patience – you must wait until the proper time."

I knew then a game was afoot. "You tease me like a silky chocolate bar waiting to be devoured," I smoothed her cheek with my fingers and kissed her for a long moment. "However, I shall wait impatiently."

"Good, nothing you do will make me tell you sooner." She giggled at my suspicion.

"No?" I finished my coffee and made clawing hands toward her. "Maybe I tickle it out of you!"

"Ahh! Every tickle makes you wait another day!" She squealed, while batting my probing fingers away.

"You win. Will you tell me before work?" I questioned with an ever-burgeoning desire to know her secret.

"Nope – patience is a virtue," she said the most devilish yet cute look.

Just then I really hated that phrase. "Alicia you are a coquettish torturer. I will be fired from making mistakes all day through puzzling out your cryptic game."

"No, you will be a good boy and earn me some money." She kissed me with an affection filled sigh. "Then the secret will be revealed."

That was it – I poked and prodded through much of the morning. Nothing I did would coerce her to tell me. So, I left for Papa's Pizzeria wondering just what I was in for. I felt this was a good secret but it could just as easily be devastating. Papa Cassio would be fed up with me by the end of the day. I'm sure more than half the pizzas I made had the wrong toppings. He only laughed when I blamed Alicia for a customer getting pineapple instead of pepperoni.

"The lady, make a mess of you, ah?" he said with a big grin while twisting his grand grey moustache.

"You have no idea. Please check all my pizzas very carefully," I told him.

"You no worry. I check very well and charge darling

Alicia for all the mistakes." Cassio whisked two perfect margaritas from the stone bake oven, sliced and served them with a sprinkling of fresh rocket. The great man jested about the secret all day. I was glad at 10 p.m. when I could finally go home and learn the secret.

The sweet smell of baking reached my nose as I entered our little apartment. "Alicia *Bello!* I've returned home to your beautiful self. May I know your secret now?" I called as I looked for her.

She came from the kitchen wearing her favourite pink apron over her favourite little green dress. "Welcome home, Gino."

"There's my teasing angel," I breathed as she reached to kiss me, allowing her Jasmine and vanilla perfume to caress my aura. Those moments always washed away the trials and tribulations of the day leaving me feeling calm and happy – except for today. "Did you have a nice day?"

"I did. I worked on my project. It'll be done in six months. I practised meditating to calm my inner child. Then I thought I'd put some of your favourite currant buns in the oven." she replied.

"My belly will be grateful." I swooped behind and kissed her neck. "However, my mind is not. It is aching with the desire to know your secret. I beg you to tell me now."

Alicia laughed on her way into the kitchen.

I followed and watched her remove the beautifully cooked buns from the oven and transfer them to a cooling rack.

"Do you really want to know?" she asked.

"I do. The suspense is killing me!" I showed her my trembling hands. They began to shake even more as she removed her apron and tossed it aside.

Dancing over to me she unzipped her dress and allowed

it to fall past her hips to the floor. Then with a kiss on my neck, she left the room.

Like a lost puppy, I followed my eyes glued to her slender, supple curves clad only in a little white bikini. "Alicia, Darling. If you wanted more fun in the bedroom; you only had to ask," I said giving her an infatuated whistle.

She shook her head. "That's not it." She stopped by the bed facing me. Running her hands down her body, she stopped at her waist.

Finally, as my heart raced and my breathing reached a feverish high; I got it. Her belly had always been flat. Now it bore a slight bump. "The buns in the oven. Calming your inner child – metaphors. You're…"

Alicia broke gave me the most beautiful smile and nodded. "I'm pregnant!"

My knees nearly failed me. That phrase was the most powerful one anyone ever spoke. I scooped Alicia up and spun her in a delighted circle. "Your gift of a child will be the greatest thing anyone has ever given to me. Thank you, Alicia."

"Are you happy?" she asked with tear-filled eyes.

"No, I'm delighted!" I told her as we fell upon the bed. There I kissed and massaged her belly. "Now we shall be a proper family. I love you, Alicia and baby."

The Delinquent Waitress

Terrance (Terry) Axum held a tight ship as the General Manager of the Riverview Hotel. He stood a tall proud man in his smart navy suit with the swan logo on the breast pocket. Terrance expected all his employees to dress in kind in their uniforms. He was a stickler for perfection and demanded everything be done just right in all the hotel's departments. He was well known for firing people who disobeyed him too. That alone garnered him a lot of respect and a little fear from his team. For the most part, they all worked hard and did a very good job. There was never a complaint about room cleanliness, food service and quality or reception service.

In the last week or so a problem had developed. The hotel restaurant's maître d'hôtel or head waiter Carlos had told him of a delinquent waitress. She'd started well and had been very good at her job. The last week or so she'd slipped in a few bad ways. Now Terry had to pull her in and deal with her.

He waited in the emerald carpeted reception until she arrived and again, she was fifteen minutes late. She looked tired and her uniform was stained and creased beneath her coat. Terry sighed and shook his head. This wouldn't do. "Amy, join me in the office, please," he said while polishing his glasses.

"Yes, Sir. Mr Axum."

He watched her head droop as she trooped passed him and beyond the counter to his office in the back hallway.

Terry entered and closed the door. A lady with a bun of carrot red hair sat behind the desk beside the general manager's big green leather chair. "I've asked the reception manager Angie to witness our meeting today to ensure it's fair for us both, okay?"

"Sure." Amy sighed and brushed her dusky-brown hair from her face with the sombreness of one going to a funeral.

Terry watched her for a moment. "Please, sit." He walked behind his desk and did the same. He made a note on Amy's report and knitted his fingers upon it as he looked at her. "As you know, this hotel is run to the highest standard. As such delinquent employees are not tolerated."

"I know, Sir." The young waitress appeared unable to look at him; instead she stared at her shaking hands in her lap.

"You've been coming in late often this last week, despite being warned by Carlos. The hotel cameras have caught you eating food from customers plates. Also, just like today, you are coming in looking unkempt and that won't do. What have you to say about that?"

"I'm guilty, fire me." Amy's shoulders began to shake as she buried her face in her hands.

Terry looked to Angie in shock; he hadn't expected this sort of reaction.

Angie's looked from the sobbing waitress to Terry. "May I?" she asked.

"Please. Amy, are you alright?" Terry asked as Angie rose and approached her.

Amy said nothing lost in her sufferance.

Angie placed an arm around her. "Aww, come on, Amy. It'll be okay. What's happened to you? I've always admired the way you used to arrive ten minutes early for work looking every bit the professional. Now, you look exhausted and why steal food when you could ask for it?"

"J-just fire me. I know y-you're going to," Amy said heaving through waves of distress.

"Shush, don't worry about that for now. Tell us what's happened, hey?" Angie said.

Terry knew Angie had a son and daughter both around

125

Amy's age. He was glad he'd asked her to sit in the meeting. "Look, Amy. I'm a stickler as a General Manager, but I'm no tyrant. I cannot and will not fire you without getting the full story. It seems to me, something tragic has befallen you and affected your work. You must tell us about it so we can help."

"I'm sorry. I shouldn't let my life affect my work." Amy's voice had gone croaky through crying.

Terry made a call and ordered water for her and coffee for everybody.

"Regardless of that, it's okay to ask for help. You could have spoken to Carlos, or even come to me if you couldn't face Terry." Angie said. "We're a team here. We'd all do what we could to help if you just asked."

"Thank you. I…"

The door opened plunging Amy into silence. A waiter called Samba came in, He'd come from Nigeria and brought a near permanent smile with him. "I bring your refreshments, sir," he said.

"Thank you, Samba." Terry beckoned him and waited as he unloaded his tray.

Samba had seen poor Amy and he stiffened. "What's going on in here? You better not be attacking or firing Amy. She is my friend and good at her job."

"It's okay, Samba. We're trying to help, Amy. That's all." Terry told him.

"Very well." Samba hugged Amy for a moment. "I got you, Amy. If they won't help – Samba will," he promised.

"Thank you, lovely," she said accepting her water. She drank thirstily as he left.

"I think you have a good friend in him," Terry said. He took a sip of his coffee. "Can you tell us what happened to you?"

"Okay, I moved here from St Ives to be with my boyfriend

Davy. Everything was going well and then a week ago I got home from work to find all my things dumped outside. Davy had found a new woman..." Amy burst into tears again bringing Angie back to her side.

"Oh, you poor thing! That's awful," she said.

"Now, I don't have a home. Davy kept my purse with my bank cards. So, I can't get back to my family in Cornwall; I can't afford food or anything and now you'll fire me as well."

"Oh, you poor girl. That's terrible," Terry said. "I'm not firing you. That would make me a terrible human being."

"Thank you, Mr Axum."

"Not at all. Where are all your belongings, now?" Terry said with a thoughtful look.

"In my car. It's parked just down the road. I ran out of fuel there. I've been sleeping in the car for the last few nights." Amy looked embarrassed and distraught at her situation.

"Why ever didn't you tell us sooner?" Angie said.

"I didn't know what to do."

"I do." Terry took a breath. "Angie, I want you to take Amy's keys and some helpers. Bring her things from her car and put them in one of the rooms." Terry took some money from his wallet. "See, if you can purchase some fuel and bring Amy's car to the hotel car park for safety as well."

"Consider it done, Terry."

"Thank you. Amy, I want you and I to visit Davy. We'll get your purse and cards from him or have him arrested for theft – his choice. You can then stay and work here at the hotel until you decide on your next move. How does that sound?"

Amy managed a smile. "I'd love that, thank you."

"Of course. Let's go and get you sorted, hey?"

The Gift of Giving

The nobleman wasn't like the others. He saw me scraping for scraps of food and gave me a half loaf of bread and an apple. I'll never forget his kind words. "You don't deserve the life of a street urchin. You are a good young lad, keep fighting and I know a better life is waiting for you. In the meantime, a gift to help you on your way. Now, chin up, lad."

With his words reverberating in my ears, I retreated from the cobblestone streets. My kind wasn't welcome here. The police would arrest and beat me if they caught me in this part of the city. The simple fact was, this area and the market were the only places I could find food. So, I'd be back same time tomorrow searching for scraps again.

With my half loaf of bread and apple cooked in my arm, I made my way toward the park. I would feast there on my way to the slum quarter I called home.

The park was your typical public area of playing fields, gravelled promenades and a pavilion for music on the weekends; all surrounded by beautiful shrubs and bushes.

I knew of a bench beneath the sycamore trees in a quiet part of the park. A place I could eat without drawing unwanted attention from those who would seek to drive me away. As I walked past the oak avenue towards the pavilion, I heard them.

"Please, Miss. My little sister and I haven't eaten in two days," begged a young lad, his trousers and shirt nothing more than rags cleaning to his skeleton.

"I hungry," the little girl offered in the most forlorn voice.

The children's pleas fell on deaf ears. The woman lifted her nose and walked away. I watched the little girl rub her belly as her brother tried again with a rich-looking man in his top hat and tails suit.

"Please, sir. Just a few coppers to buy bread. Please, help—"

The man lashed out, catching the boy with a vicious backhanded blow across the face. "How dare you beg from me. Get away from me you filthy, disgusting, boy!"

I was already on the move as the man raised the foot to assault him again. "The boy means no harm. You have no right to hurt him!" I yelled as I stepped between them.

"Maybe, it's you I should teach a lesson to. I'd bet you taught these beggars how to make money from strangers, didn't you?" The man's face reddened as he rolled back his sleeves in readiness to fight.

"No, but if it is the only way they can eat, then they have little choice. I will not fight you. Take your riches and be gone, snob!"

The man huffed and raised his nose. "Fine! I'm going, I can't stand the stench around here this afternoon," he said before stalking away.

"Thank you, sir," said the young boy extending a hand.

I shook it with a smile. "I'm no sir. I'm a street urchin just like the two of you. May I know your names?"

"I Carrie, he Edwin," answered the little girl.

"Nice to meet you, Carrie and Edwin. Come," I beckoned them and began to sing.

♫ *Walk a mile with me*
   Oh, the good things you'll see
   A happy little sunset
   The princess in her parapet ♫

Pausing, I gently poked her nose drawing the giggle.

"You have a lovely voice," said Edwin.

I nodded my thanks.

♫ *Walk a mile with me*
We'll be home in time for tea
Let's walk until the parish ends
Won't you join me, my friends ♫

"We will," Carrie said smiling at me as if I was some kind of magician.

I led them to my bench under the sycamore trees. A squirrel scarpered as we drew near. Mr Robin stayed on his branch to watch.

"Sit a while," I offered, patting the bench. It was then I looked at the apple and the bread still cooked in my arm. What good are possessions if you don't share them, right?

"What's your name?" asked Edwin.

"They call me Rupert. Here." I tore the bread into three chunks and gave the children the two largest bits.

"Edwin, we okay eat?"

The boy looked to his sister and then up to me for an answer.

"Go on, you eat every crumb. Enjoy it little one." I ruffled her messy blonde hair as I ate some of my bread.

"Thank you, Mr Rupert," Edwin mumbled through a mouthful of bread. He was scoffing it like a hungry dog and enjoying every bite.

"My pleasure," I assured him as I took out a pocket-knife I'd stolen from a market stall long ago. I divided the apple into three. Again, I gave Edwin and Carrie the largest pieces. My own immutable hunger wouldn't recede today. At least the children wouldn't be quite so hungry. As I watched them eat the little food I'd possessed for all of twenty minutes, I smiled. The simple act of kindness shown to me by the nobleman provided me with food. I'd mirrored his generosity with the children and for that, I'd been rewarded a moment of contentment and happiness.

"Yes, giving a little is worth so much more."

The Hollow Ballerina

Her silk-white dancing slippers were a whirl as she skimmed the polished floorboards, twirling through magical arabesque and fouetté poses. Cameras flashed and the audience applauded, the music dipped and slowed. She was one of two dozen ballerinas on stage but she felt so alone. With statuesque elegance, she followed the rhythm with her bobbing plié; rising upon tiptoe with a masterful passé. The drums hit an invigorating height. She flew like a graceful crane, a magnificent grand-jete split and the most delicate, magnificent landing left her heart humming in her chest. She could feel the excitement in her troupe, but every time she faced the audience her energy and her spirit plummeted. Although she never missed a beat, filled the stage with perfect balance, poise and gracefulness, her heart was heavy. The crescendo hit, she pranced a pirouette around the Prima Ballerina, leapt aloft and landed in a perfect split with her arms held high. The curtain dropped to raucous applause. Clapping hands were muffled by the pounding of her heart in her ears. The muted footfalls of her soft slippers told of her fleeing the stage as the lights went out. Friendly voices called her name, each worried for her. She ignored them all in favour of solitude. To be alone with her tears was all she desired.

She went into a quiet dressing room, kicked off her ballet slippers and hauled the itchy chiffon of her dress over and away from her neck. Tearing the barrettes from her glossy chestnut hair, she slumped upon the white sofa. Her head turned to the window, her eyes seeing nothing but visions of that which tore at her heart. Hugging her knees, she allowed her tears to fall like little diamonds in the light as they splashed onto the lace skirts of her dress.

"When the next matinee comes, I will be there to watch you dance, Cherub," he'd promised.

"You mean that?" She'd asked, so happy to hear those words. Knowing he was showing an interest in her ballet meant everything to her.

"Every word. You've proven me very wrong and so I shall honour that with my presence this coming Wednesday."

And so, believing him, she'd practised harder than ever before. As the matinee curtain lifted, she'd danced her heart out and yet his seat was empty. The curtains had closed on her greatest performance, her passion extinguished with the lights on the stage.

She was so lost in her heartbreak and as forlorn as the most sunless cellar. She never heard her door open. Her guest's soft footsteps lost to her sobs.

"Dear Adaline, you danced like the most magnificent gazelle. You shone brighter than the Prima Ballerina herself. They're calling you "La Ballerine Angélique" out there. And yet here you are, sobbing as if you alone ruined the show. Please, what makes you so sad?"

Adaline felt a hand gently massaging her bare shoulder. "Thank you, Martina. My heart was broken this afternoon. I cannot dance like an angel anymore…" Adaline paused to control her tears and slipped her dress over her neck to hide her modesty. "If I were to dance again, I would become La Ballerine Creuse and your show does not deserve that."

"The hollow ballerina? But why dear, Adaline. You have been practising for La Princesse Enchantée, haven't you?"

"I have." Adaline shook her head amid fresh tears. "Lily deserves a passionate ballerina to be her maid, not a miserable flop like I shall be."

"Why, no, dear Adaline. Lily is a beautiful ballerina, of course. Yet after your mesmerising performance today, if she is cast as La Princesse, the Ballet shall be a flop, never you."

132

Adaline lifted her face to the friendly stage manager. Her eyes reddened, swollen from crying. Her delicate makeup tarnished by the track marks of falling tears. "What are you saying, Martina?"

"You are my enchanted princess. The winter ballet will be the best our theatre has ever held, but only with you as my Prima Ballerina." Martina grinned at her but his pleasure faded fast.

Adaline shook her head. "I'm sorry, Martina. But I cannot."

"Why?"

"I—" Adaline heard the door bang against the wall. Turning to see who'd thundered in, her mouth dropped open in surprise.

"Pardon my blundering intrusion," said the gentleman entering the dressing room. He stood tall and handsome in his finest black suit. A single yellow rose was held in his right hand. "I think I know the answer to your question."

"Papa… "Adaline tried to say more but fresh tears prevented her words from flowing.

"I'm here, Cherub." He came and knelt beside the sofa, taking and kissing her hand. "Those tears and the desire not to dance are for me, aren't they?"

Adaline nodded as he reached and tenderly dried her eyes with a handkerchief. "You promised to watch me perform and yet your seat was bare."

"I know, but I was here. I watched my beautiful daughter perform in a way, only angels can. Even the Prima Ballerina looked like a trainee in the shadow of the magical light you brought to that stage. You were magnificent and I am so very proud of you, my daughter."

"Thank you, Papa, So, where were you?" Adaline was shaking now, her body tingling with rising elation.

"I had a run-in with a constable and arrived as the

curtain rose. The ushers forced me to sit at the very back. I was still close enough to be in awe of my wonderful daughter." He held out the rose. "Adaline, Martina has given you a wonderful opportunity this winter. Will you be the Enchanted Princess on stage?"

Adaline wiped her eyes again. Her heart was thrumming in her chest. Her Papa had seen her dance and loved it. Her face lit up with the most beautiful smile and she nodded as she took the rose and smelled it. "I shall."

"Then, Cherub. I promise to be in the front row for as many shows as I can."

Adaline rose to her feet and allowed him to dance her into a warm hug. "I'd love that, Papa." Turning to Martina she hugged him too. "Thank you, Martina. I shall never be the hollow ballerina again now my Papa is here."

"You never were, dear Adaline." Martina kissed her forehead with a fond smile. "You have always been an angel in ballet slippers. Now, you shall prove it to the world."

The Old Man in the Park

Anne Clements worked at the Freesia Florists by the park. She'd been an assistant there for three months now. Every lunchtime she'd take a walk in the park and eat her sandwiches by the rock-walled koi pond. Not a single day passed without her seeing old Bob standing by the water.

Today was no different. There he was with his black cowboy hat parked on his clouds of white hair, and beard that matched. He stood a plaintive man in his old black suit with a red-and-white bouquet under his arm and a black guitar over his shoulder. As always he was just standing and staring at the meadow beyond the pond.

He was a mystery to Anne. She didn't even know if his name was Bob. She just called him such to be more respectful than "old man". The enigma only deepened for her when realising the Freesia Florist was the only place to buy flowers near the park; and yet she'd never served him in her three months. Even her boss said she'd never seen him.

Anne hoped he was planning to sing one day – what with his guitar over his shoulder. Even if he sounded bad, she'd was eager to hear his song. Yet three months to the day she first saw him, he was yet to move a muscle during lunch break. Smiling, she thought he made the most interesting and yet boring mime, a still yet bloody good statue.

Watching Bob today, Anne realised, not one person acknowledged him as they walked by. They didn't even seem to see him. Had they grown so used to seeing the enigmatic man that he'd become part of the scenery?

Having finished lunch, Anne came to a decision. She'd go and try to chat to him, maybe solve the puzzle if she could.

She brushed crumbs from her clothes, gathered her things and stood. A mother and her two children passed by before she could approach Bob. The little boy seemed to glance at him but only for a second as his mother ushered him on.

"Excuse me. My name's Anne. I work at the florist over there."

The old man blinked and turned his head to face her but said nothing.

"I see you standing here looking so sad every day. Is there anything I can do to help?" Anne tried, determined to connect with him.

A smile graced his lips as he gave the smallest nod. "You already do. You're the only person who notices me, the first to talk to me in thirty years."

Anne felt a little shock at his reply. "You mean, you stood here every day for three decades?"

A gentleman in a blue suit scowled at her as he passed by.

"Much longer than that dear, lady," said the old man.

"But whatever for?" Anne couldn't comprehend the situation. What would compel anybody to stand in the park every day for their whole life?

The old man took a step back towards the water. Taking a red bloom from his flowers, he pointed towards a stone at his feet.

Anne followed his direction and gasped. There was writing carved into the stone. It was hard to read with so much lichen and weathering. Using the lid of her flask she scooped water from the pond, poured it over the inscription and began to read.

On this spot in 1921, a runaway car killed long-time park busker Mr Bob Earsham as he waited to mark his wedding to his new wife Pearl. This stone bears memory to the wonderful, kind, entertainer he was. May he rest in peace.

"I've been waiting a long time to give these flowers to Pearl," Bob said. "I'll stand here as long as it takes."

Overcome with sadness, Anne wiped her eyes. She had no idea how she knew his name was Bob before today. At least now she had a reason why people walk passed without seeing him. "Oh, Bob lovely. She's not going to come to you. I'm sorry to tell you, you passed away in 1921. You died, sweetheart."

Bob looked down at the stone and sighed. "So, that thing tells the truth then?"

"I'm afraid it does." Anne pulled out her phone and used the internet to search for Pearl Earsham. It didn't take her long to find some information. "Look, I found your wife. She made it to the age of ninety and passed away in eight-nine."

Bob looked at the phone and smiled as tears flowed into his fluffy beard. "There she is. There's my beautiful, Pearl."

"Would you like to see her again?" Anne asked.

"Oh, very much." Bob looked hopeful.

"Do you see the bright white light somewhere around you?"

Bob looked over the Koi pond and nodded. "It's there. I hear harpsichord music coming from it. The light scares me."

"Oh, please don't be afraid. Beyond that light is heaven. I promise, Pearl is waiting on the other side for you."

"She is?"

"Yes, Bob. You go on through now. Be with her and rest. You deserve it, sweety." Anne wiped her eyes again and glared at a headshaking onlooker passing by. They couldn't see nor understand.

"Okay." Bob nodded. "Thank you for helping me, Anne. May your life be one of happiness."

Anne watched him turn and vanish into the air. That was the last time she'd see him standing in the park with his flowers and guitar. A day later a bouquet of red roses and white lilies with a little guitar arrived at the florist's addressed to her. There was no gift givers name but Anne smile; these flowers, she knew, were heaven-sent.

The Recovery Man

"Dillon, we've got a single female driver in a broken down Megane soft top. She's on the hard shoulder of the motorway. Five miles southbound beyond the Longway's Services."

"Roger that, Sue. Let's not leave alone her for too long. I'm on my way." Dillon grinned as he pulled his recovery truck out of the services and accelerated with the traffic. He loved nothing more than to improve people's days by getting their vehicles going again. "Did she give any more details?" he asked over the radio.

"She says; the car just died. Don't be horrible to her if she's run out of fuel will you."

"Never! I always do my best to help my customers avoid embarrassment and keep every last vestige of respect they can." Dillon settled into the drive while keeping his eyes firmly on the big rigs passing him in the fast lane. Those and the maniac speeders kept him on his toes.

This afternoon was passing in a calm fashion. Maybe it was the sunny day affording the drivers relaxed energy on their commutes. Dillon glanced in his rear-view mirror and grinned to himself. He'd allowed a moustache to sprout on his upper lip in the last few weeks. His wife hated it, but he thought it looked handsome.

The orange emergency beacons on the Megane soon came into view. Dillon engaged his recovery lights, indicated and pulled on to the shoulder behind the sky-blue car. He stopped his recovery truck thirty-feet behind his customer. There it provided a little warning and protective cover from the seventy-mile-an-hour traffic.

An oil tanker thundered by shaking the recovery truck. Dillon took a deep breath, opened his door and slipped out with his tablet in hand. This part of the job was always an adrenaline rush. Working close to the live lanes was taking his life into his hands. It was exhilarating and scary all at once. With the appearance of a six-foot-tall safety cone in his orange coveralls, he walked to the car and tapped on the driver's window. He gave a cheery smile and spoke once it was wound down, "Good afternoon, madam. I'm Dillon. I'll soon get you going again," he announced himself loudly over the passing vehicles.

"Thank you for coming so quickly. I'm Jessica and this old car's giving me a headache!" She looked relieved to see him.

"Pleased to meet you, Jessica." Dillon checked her details and noted some more about the vehicle. He noticed the young blonde lady was wearing a skimpy white dress and feeling uncomfortable by the way she was covering herself with her arms. "Okay, so what happened?" he asked while respectfully averting his eyes.

"I was on my way to the New Life Spa Resort. I won a weekend there you see." Jessica began.

"Oh, very nice. I might join you for a shoulder massage, later on." Dillon chuckled as he kept his eyes off her by watching the passing traffic.

"Well, you would deserve it if you get me going again."

"Rest assured I'm not leaving you until you have a working car, or I get you somewhere safe. What happened with this old girl?" Dillon placed a hand on the black fabric roof and turned away from a cloud of dust belching from a fast-moving curtain side lorry.

"Well, I don't really know. First, the dashboard lights started blinking and going out. Then everything just died. I coasted onto the hard shoulder and managed to stop safely. Now, it won't even start." Jessica told him with a frustrated flap of her hands. "It is fixable isn't it?"

Dillon recorded her version of events on his tablet. "No

worries, I reckon we can get you going again. Can you pop the bonnet and turn the key for me?"

"Sure," Jessica leaned over and pulled the lever causing the bonnet to jump on its latch.

Dillon made to step around the front and flinched as a horn blared loud in his ears. He swore and squashed himself flat against the car. A double-decker car transport lorry shrieked by missing his belly by less than an inch. "Get over you, bloody idiot!" Dillon yelled shaking his fist angrily.

"Wow! Are you okay?" asked Jessica aghast.

"I'm fine, thanks. I nearly lost 6 inches of belly quicker than one of those new keto diets then though," Dillon chuckled as he moved to open the bonnet. "Okay, try to start her up please!"

"It's still not doing anything?"

The recovery driver raised a hand. He'd heard the starter motor click but nothing else happened. A glance about the clean engine bay told him the car was well maintained. There was only one thing this could be. "Looks like your battery's knackered. I'll grab my engine starter and we'll find out."

"Thank you," Jessica blushed and looked away toward the fields.

"My pleasure," Dillon diced with death as he walked back along the shoulder to his recovery truck. He soon had the tools he needed and quickly wired up the battery. "Right, try and start her again," he instructed.

This time as Jessica turned the key her car spluttered into life. "Hey! It worked. You're a genius."

Dillon had already began winding his cables away. When he was done, he closed the bonnet again. "Just call me Dillon Einstein!" He flashed a smile and chuckled. "Right, if you stall or turn the engine off it probably won't start again. Drive down to the next roundabout and go right.

141

Two miles down, there's a left turn into an industrial estate. Pull in there. The red building as you drive in, is a car parts place that'll have the battery you need."

"What if I have to stop along the long way," Jessica's faced taughtened with fear.

"Don't you worry. I'm going to follow you there and change that battery for you. I'll flash my indicators when I'm ready. Then you can pick up speed on the hard shoulder and join the traffic when safe."

"You're an angel, Dillon."

"And you're too kind. See you in a few minutes." Dillon swiftly loaded his gear back into his truck and indicated for her to drive on. Fortune favoured him today. Jessica was a good driver; she negotiated the roundabout and the five-mile journey without a hitch. Dillon went straight into the spare parts store to purchase a new battery. When he came back the Megane was there but Jessica wasn't.

With growing concern, Dillon put the battery by the car and walked from the car park to find her. A look about left him smiling; she was heading down the path with an arm full of goodies from Sam's Food truck. "There you are, I thought some rotten bugger had abducted you then!"

"So, sorry I scared you," Jessica smiled appreciatively. "I saw the food truck and an opportunity. I didn't know what you liked, so I bought coffee, bacon rolls and some doughnuts to thank you for helping me."

Dillon took the coffees as they walked back to her car. "That's the loveliest thing a customer has ever done for me," he said.

"Aww, well you deserve it for risking your life to save others."

"My wife would disagree. She wants me to become a postman or something. She reckons I'm selfish risking my life for others when she's waiting for me at home." Dillon accepted a bacon roll and began to eat while changing out the defective battery.

"I think that's quite romantic," Jessica told him from the driver's seat.

"Yeah, I suppose it is." Dillon tightened the last bolt and connected the positive and negative terminals. "Righto, start her up again."

Jessica turned the key and the car jumped into life. "Woohoo! She's alive again!" she said with delight.

"Mission complete. The spa awaits dear lady." Dillon shut the bonnet for her and came around to the driver's door. "Can you just read the screen and sign at the bottom for me? This just verifies what I did and that I got you going again. You will receive all the details by email should you need to make enquiries, complaints or anything."

"Why would I need to complain?" Jessica read swiftly and signed. "You helped me like the perfect gentleman."

"You'd be surprised by some of the complaints we receive. I helped a young fiancé a while back. In his hurry to get to the alter he curbed his car puncturing two tyres. I drove him to church, then went back to change his tyres and towed his car to church for him. Yet, he still complained that it was my fault he was late for his wedding!"

"Really? What a stupid man!" Jessica stood up and kissed Dillon on the cheek. "I think I was a lucky lady being rescued by you. I'll be telling your boss that you're my hero."

"It was my pleasure you have a safe journey and a wonderful weekend now." Dillon shut her car door and waved as she drove away. The warm feeling in his heart at knowing he'd rescued Jessica was why he did this job. Helping people safely on their way was the most rewarding thing he'd ever done.

The Smokejumper's Miracle

He'd fallen a thousand feet through moody skies, having jumped from a short C-23 Sherpa plane. A tug on his ripcord sent his red parachute billowing above him. Dustin knew he'd completed the safest part of his job as he dropped through the smoky air. Below, the pine forest had the appearance of a horror movie. Thick smoke and flames lashed the air, pouring from the canopy in several locations. A stray cigarette started the blaze and now winds had spread and distributed the inferno over many miles of the forest.

Dustin proudly called himself a smokejumper – a flying firefighter. With a hundred pounds of gear strapped to him, he leapt into the danger zone to combat blazes in unreachable places. Today's mission was to head the fire off before it hit a power station.

Dustin scanned the sky and smiled as he picked out his six teammates descending in a long line.

Then he was in the trees. He yanked his cord, aiming for a clearing, kicked off a tree branch and rolled to a safe landing. He hauled the parashoot off, and shoved it in his pack.

The heat was tremendous already and he wasn't near the flames. He took a second to get his helmet comfortable on his sweating head, took up his axe, glanced at his GPS unit and broke into a run.

On his chest, his radio crackled to life. "Dustin, you good?"

"Affirmative, Clive. On route to position now."

"Roger that, good luck."

"Thanks, just get some beers in the fridge will yer." Dustin ducked some low branches and increased his pace.

"Consider it done. Clive out."

The radio went silent. Dustin saw deer, squirrels and birds all crossing his path, each desperate to escape the coming inferno. Even as he watched, a tree to the east burst into flames. Its dry wood erupting with terrifying speed.

With a deep nerve-controlling breath, Dustin jogged through billowing clouds of smoke and ash, following the fire line north. He was almost at his section of the firebreak. He was to cut down trees and pull bushes to create a long wide clearing. Then by back burning, he and the team hoped to extinguish the advancing fire by eliminating its fuel.

Dustin leapt a fallen tree, his chainsaw clunking over it. With a crack of twigs, he landed on one knee and felt his attention drawn. He snapped around to the east and gasped; black as night with smoke, the sky pulsed boiling red with fire. That wasn't his main concern, not far away a cabin in the smouldering trees. A girl was sitting on the doorstep. The inferno was burning closer with every passing second.

"Oh, shit! Clive, I got kids out here!"

"Kids? Damn it, man. Tell 'em to get out of there and start fire-breaking – there's no time."

"Will do." Dustin banked left; he wasn't leaving the kids to die. He dashed through a line of trees into the cabin's clearing. Water butt right of the door– that'll be handy. The girl was gone, the door open. Skirting a fire pit, Dustin ran straight inside. There looking terrified were two boys and the girl, none older than ten.

"Have you seen our daddy?" asked the girl.

"Sorry, where'd he go? What're your names?" Dustin glanced around the cabin and did not like what he saw.

"Daddy went to see if we could get out. He didn't come back. I'm Brad, he's Mikey and she's Sarah," replied the eldest boy.

"Okay, don't worry. We'll find him." Dustin relayed

the information to base his eyes on the large propane tank and the box of shotgun shells. This place was like a giant frag grenade.

"Please help us," Sarah said tearfully.

"I will. We—" Dustin watched the back of the cabin ignite. Flames ripped through the log wall and the children screamed. "Everybody outside now!" Dustin scooped up Mikey the youngest and dashed to the door.

"The trees are burning!" yelled Brad pointing.

"I see them," Dustin gulped. The trees all around the clearing were now ablaze. He and the kids were trapped. "Clive, I need a water drop at my position. We're stuck in a ring of flame with a cabin full of explosives on fire." Dustin radioed.

No response came back.

"Flamin' hell!" Dustin burst into action. He grabbed covers from the bed seconds before they were incinerated. He doused them in water from a butt outside and re-joined the kids.

"What are you doing?" Sarah asked.

"Whatever I can. Put this around you and huddle by the fire pit." Dustin pulled on his breathing mask and shot into the cabin. Full of smoke and flames it was a choking inferno now. Unseen things popped, crackled and hissed as the fire destroyed them. He sent the ammo box sliding toward the door and swiftly disconnected the propane tank. Shouldering it, he burst out of the smoke and dumped the propane in the water butt. The shotgun shells followed it. The water might stop them detonating – he hoped.

"The fire's getting closer!" Mikey screamed pointing at a Douglas fir fully ablaze.

"I see it, pal." Dustin found himself gritting his teeth as he turned a circle, taking in the hundred-foot high walls of flames all around him. *We need a bloody miracle to get out of this.*

A flash of light came from the cabin. Dustin ran at the kids and shoved them to the ground. An earth-shaking bang sent flames and smoke crackling into the sky. Debris cascaded to earth all around the four. There was another noise from high above too, one that brought hope.

"Kids, you okay?" Dustin shook the remains of the door frame and wood splinters from his back and stood up.

"Yeah, what the hell was that?" Sarah pulled Mikey's wet blanket around him again.

"I missed something explosive inside, I reckon." Dustin glanced at the cabin's remains, boiling with fire. The propane tank and shells were no longer in the butt. It was gone.

Something cracked close at hand.

"MOVE!" Dustin grabbed Mikey and pushed the others away. The fir tree fell, slamming to earth with a roar of flames right where they'd been standing.

"That was…"

Lightning flashed across the angry sky with stunning pizzazz of blue, red and white light.

"…too close!" Brad finished as thunder rumbled and crackled above them.

"No kidding! Come on you, beauty – rain!" Dustin glanced aloft, then at the propane tank. Flames were creeping upon it now. Better still raindrops were fizzing onto the hot metal. Within seconds the storm began a tumultuous downpour upon the forest. Dustin beamed in relief, laughed, as it washed the soot from his face and extinguished some of the fires.

"It's raining like a gift from heaven," Sarah said.

"It sure is. Let's get out of here," Dustin urged as forks of lightning split the sky above the smoking trees. An hour of walking saw them meeting with paramedics and ground fire crews. Dustin left the kids in their capable hands and plunged back into the forest to ensure the powerplant was saved and the fires would be extinguished.

He and the team would have to fight for a few more days but the majestic rumbling storm would surely help them as much as it had saved Dustin and the kids. Their father would be found, alive, a day later. In the weeks which followed, Dustin wearing his fine and glamourous dress-suit, stood full of a different type of pizzazz. He was awarded a hero's medal for saving Sarah, Mikey and Brad – his new best friends.

Start and Prevail

The Aerodrome race track was cloaked in misty rain. The roar of engines signalled the start of a not-so-legal race. This was a street racing competition with racers driving turbocharged Mazda, Nissan and Subaru cars. Each visible by its neon lights and the flames kicking out of its exhaust as it hurtled around the track.

In the black Nizmo with red neon lights was Wes. The fear in his eyes told of more than a race at stake. He gunned his accelerator and drifted past a Scooby. He'd given-up street racing when he turned twenty-one. Now at almost fifty, he was forced back behind the wheel. He needed the two-hundred-and-fifty grand prize money to save his twelve-year-old daughter, Maddie. She'd been diagnosed with a rare cancer and only specialist treatment in Switzerland could save her. This race was Wes's only chance get her that life-saving treatment.

Hitting the straight, he shot-up through the gears and powered into fifth place. Fiery torches, phone lights, loud music and cheering reached his ears over the roaring engines as he whipped by the stands.

Ahead, the violet Mazda and blue Scooby in the third and fourth were jousting for position. Sparks flew as the two collided and bounded apart into the hard-right bend. The Scooby oversteered and entered the gravel, only to lurch back onto the track.

"Crazy fools, this isn't a destruction derby." Wes braked a touch, made it around the bend, and then hit the turbo to regain his one-hundred-and-forty miles per hour speed. As the track straightened he swore.

Something exploded ahead.

The violet Mazda slewed across the track, its lights going out as it smashed into the Scooby and flew high into the air.

149

Wes swore, his car going right under the flying Mazda as the Scooby thundered off the track and buried itself in the tire wall. Wes glanced in his rear-view mirror to see an explosion of flames as the Mazda impacted the track behind him. "Bloody hell!"

"Racers, the collision will not end this race. Be mindful of the debris and get over that finish line," came the order over the drivers' headsets.

"Wes fixed his eyes ahead and set his jaw. "Right on!" he sucked in a breath, hurtled around the next bend. He eased up to one-fifty miles per hour and reeled in the yellow Silvia in second. It was twenty years newer than the Nizmo. Yet Wes smiled; with the modifications his car was carrying, he should catch it alright.

Two bends later they were hood to hood and grappling for second place. The Silvia's driver Conan couldn't resist flipping Wes off as they roared down the back straight.

Wes laughed at him and took a position for the coming bend. A little gas saw him nudge ahead as he punched the handbrake and screeched into the bend sideways.

Conan had gone in straighter and tighter.

Wes thumped back in his seat, the Silvia slammed into his rear bumper slewing him off course. Gravel hammered against the underside of the car, as he dropped down the gears, gained traction and fired back onto the track. "You'll pay for that, Conan!" he yelled as they raced through an S-bend and back toward the pitlanes.

Once more, Wes used his turbo to catch-up. He came alongside Conan's Silvia and wound down his window. "Hey, pal. Looks like you need a break!" he yelled over the roaring engines.

"No chance!" Conan gave a two-fingered salute.

"Goodbye!" Wes had been easing past him. At the last moment, he jinked the wheel left and crunched into the

150

Silvia. Glass broke and a wing-mirror vanished as Conan's car disappeared into the pitlane, spinning like a top.

Wes refocused on the track. He was sweating and trembling with adrenaline. "Last lap. If I catch the last car, I can save Maddie. Come on, Wes! You have to do this!" he told himself as he sped passed the flaming barrels around the stands of cheering fans.

There was the gold Skyline. Easily the fastest car on the track, Wes gained but slowly. On the deep bend out of the front straight, he punched the clutch and came around it sharply, back on the accelerator and turbo he caught up dramatically. Kicking up debris from the crash earlier, he swore. His windscreen crazed, making it difficult to see.

The gold Skyline's brakes came on ahead. The last driver had seen the wrecked Mazda on its side – late. The Skyline was forced to slow left the track to avoid a collision.

Wes grinned as he powered through a haze of smoke and twisted metal leaving the wreckage behind.

The Skyline was only three car lengths ahead now.

Wes saw the next bend coming fast, he popped the handbrake, drifted around the curve and flashed through the gears as fast as he could.

Two car lengths gap between the cars now.

Nothing changed on the back straight, or the next bend. It was in the S-bend that Wes's superior drifting helped him. He whizzed in and out of the turns without losing a beat. He reeled in the Skyline and drew level with it. A look left gave him a shock. "Erica!" He and Erica had been lovers when he raced years ago. Apparently, she'd never stopped racing.

The blonde racer looked his way and gaped.

Wes's headset crackled. "Wes, why are you racing again?" she asked as they raced on neck and neck.

"My daughter damn it." Wes felt tears burning his eyes as he urged his car onward.

"Shit, your daughter's Maddie in the paper, isn't she?" Erica replied.

The two cars roared passed the pitlanes.

Only one bend and a half the straight to the flag.

"Yeah, that's her. She's dying damn it." Wes set himself and hurled his car around the bend.

Erica had the upper hand, she accelerated passed and blocked his route forward. "I'm sorry…"

Wes heard the headset click off. He pulled wide and floored his car but Erica was winning the race. He shook his head no chance now—

The Skyline had come within feet of the finish line. It braked, went into a donut slide and flashed passed Wes.

He gaped as his eyes met Erica's streaming with tears as he passed her and crossed the finish line first. By some miracle, he'd won his most important race ever.

"Why'd you let me win, Erica?" he asked once he caught up with her outside the track later.

"I can win any race I want. I'll make my money next time. Take your purse for winning this one and save your daughter, okay?" Erica hugged him. "I want to see her fit and well in the papers soon."

"You're a hero, Erica. I promise to bring her to thank you personally." Wes wiped his eyes as he looked at the winners cheque grasped in his shaking hand.

"Nah, I just did the right thing. You're the hero racing for your daughter. Now bugger off and give her the good news." Erica grinned as she climbed into her car and roared away.

Wes looked at the stars above his head and said, "Thank you!"

Theatrical Justice

A raucous orchestral tune filled a room. Joel took a deep breath as he drew his strong, lean body tall before the mirror. He imagined himself in a full prince's costume as he prepared to sing.

A thunderous bang rattled the mirror. It was followed by a hammering and then the burr of a very loud drill.

"For goodness sake!" Joel snapped the music off and turned to leave the room. He knew the overhaul of the stage was a necessary evil. For the upcoming show to shine, the stage had to look its best. This still didn't excuse them sounding like they were demolishing the bloody building all day.

Joel grabbed his rucksack and heard his phone trilling inside. Retrieving it, he saw a message waiting:

Sorry, Joel. Cassie quit. Come and see me immediately, Dennis.

Cursing his luck, Joel dashed from the practice room and cannoned straight into somebody running down the corridor in a marshmallow-pink dress.

"I-I'm sorry!" The ballerina let out a sob and made to run away.

"Hey, there's no harm done." Joel took in her sleek bronze bun of hair and the pretty shape her dress gave her. "Are you, okay?"

"Sorry – I…" she glanced back and stumbled into the wall in her haste to escape.

Joel caught her arm and steadied her with a smile. "Slow down and take a deep breath for a moment, hey. You know, I don't think we've met." Joel frowned as he admired her. "I'm sure I'd recognise somebody with the beautiful hair and stunning topaz eyes you possess. May I know your name?"

153

"I'm Saphira." She blushed. "Thank you for the compliment."

"Nice to meet you, Saphira." Joel introduced himself and led the way down the corridor. "Now, we know each other, can you tell me why you were crying. I'd like to help you if I can."

"No, I don't want to burden you."

"Please. I insist."

"Okay." Saphira took a deep breath. "I've been practising for my first show. I made friends with another ballerina called Irina. Anyway, our producer Darius told her that she had to work harder or she'd lose her lead role and I'd get it because I was doing better."

"It was naughty of Darius to say something like that publicly. Still, it's a good thing for you, right?"

"You'd think so, but no. It cost me my role in the show." Saphira let herself be led into the theatre's lunchroom as her tears flowed again.

"What? Why, if you're doing so well?" Joel made two mugs of tea and sat down with her. "Here, drink this. Why are you no longer in the show?"

"Thanks." Saphira took a sip and composed herself. "Irina did it. She sabotaged me. She found a way to convince Darius that I was just trying to get the lead role to ruin the show. He wouldn't listen to me when I tried to defend myself and fired me from the production. Eliza, another dancer, reckons he's going to tell Dennis what happened so I... I can never perform here again."

The story left Joel feeling flabbergasted; he couldn't believe such atrocities could happen within the theatre. Seeing Saphira crying, he gave her a comforting rub of the shoulder. "That's awful! I'm so sorry that happened to you. I—" Joel flicked his eyes to his phone and fell silent for a thoughtful moment. "Sorry... Look, I'm going to help you sort this out."

"Really?" Saphira gave him a hopeful look and dried her eyes. "How can you do that?"

"Can you sing?"

"Yes, I do choir and singing practice two nights a week and dancing practice the other three. Why?"

Joel smiled at Saphira's quizzical expression. "That's amazing dedication to your art. Do you know the song *Fairytale Dream* from the musical of the same name?"

Saphira nodded and broke into a smile. "I love that song. I even watched you perform it on the training stage with Cassie Blake." Looking around her she took a deep breath and closed her eyes.

> ♫ *In my fairy tale dream,*
> *There's a handsome prince for me.*
> *An angelic man*
> *His kiss will set me free.* ♫

Joel couldn't help a beaming smile on his face. Saphira sang the power ballad with a natural grace which filled him with electrically charged energy. As she finished her stanza, he followed with his the next; filling the room with his rich, deep voice.

> ♫ *There is our fairy tale princess?*
> *Will my dreams come true?*
> *Is she to be my, Eleanor*
> *My heart beats for you!* ♫

The two sang the rest of the song together with Saphira finishing beautifully. "Aww, I loved that," she said with a little blush to her cheeks.

"Splendida! I must say, that was amazing!" Remarked a gentleman making himself a coffee.

Joel recognised him as Gregorio the orchestra conductor. "Saphira was divine, wasn't she?"

"Tu es magnifica, Saphira." Gregorio kissed her hand and whistled as he left.

"He's charming." Saphira grinned as she sipped her tea. "So, why did you have me sing the—"

"Not so you could perform it. You'll never perform here again!" snapped a feminine voice.

Joel turned to see another ballerina enter. "You must be Irina?" Seeing her nod, he continued, "Whether Saphira performs here again or not is nothing to do with you. I think you trying to end her career is despicable. That said, do join me for my opening show on August fifteenth, won't you?"

Irina huffed, took a bottle of orange juice from the vending machine and pranced out.

"Ha! I think you upset her," Saphira chuckled.

"Good." Joel finished his tea and stood. "Come with me. We have a meeting with Dennis to attend.

Eight days later the theatre's overhaul was complete. The auditorium was full of people decked out in beautiful suits and dresses. They applauded as a drum roll prompted the velvet curtains to open. Joel entered the stage in his role as the gardener. Humming, he began to tend his bed of plants as he broke into a song about flowers. Around him, dancers dressed as the blooms made the show colourful and spectacular. Amid them, a stagecoach pulled by beautiful white horses entered centre stage. Princess Eleanor emerged wearing a beautiful red dress. She was none other than Saphira and was unable to hide just how proud and happy she was to be performing with Joel. She perched in the garden and began her love affair with Joel's character as she sang about the beautiful day. During her performance, she couldn't help but notice Irina. The scornful ballerina had

156

left her seat in the audience and run from the auditorium in floods of tears.

This night it would be Saphira enjoying the spotlight and the applause alongside her hero Joel.

True Treasures

"It's no good, Burt. That old tree has to go," complained Edna for the twelfth day in a row.

Burt gazed over his garden and nodded. The trees were all beautifully green except that one old alder. It served solely as a perch for the crows these days. There was one of the cunning black birds there now; according to his tilting head movements, he was scheming ways to get his beak on the last sandwich on the table. Burt sighed, there was no way to tiptoe around it, the sharp frosts of winter had finally killed the alder. "Yup, time it's laid to rest before it falls on somebody," he conceded.

"Glad you agree. You get the chainsaw. I'll make some tea." Edna's knees crunched as she rose from her patio chair and went indoors.

"That's it, go on! You do the easy bit – I'll do the hard work as usual!" Burt grumbled after her as he disappeared into the shed.

It wasn't long before the staccato roaring of the chainsaw echoed around the village. Under Burt's guidance, it bit into and sawed a notch in the old trunk. The crow cawed his displeasure from atop a neighbouring tree.

"I know, fella. You don't have to listen to my missus every day if I leave this tree here," Burt told the black-feathered bird while repositioning his saw.

A final cut saw the tree drop neatly onto the lawn. There was one casualty – the tree swiped the bird table on the way down.

"Bloody hell, Burt! You broke my sodding birdfeeder. Can't you do anything right!" Edna nagged having brought out the tea.

"Tell you what, I'll go watch the horseracing. You finish up out here," he replied.

"No – no, you started, so you can finish, now." Edna scooped up the broken feeder and headed back indoors.

Burt stood and sipped his tea. "You see, crow, I can never do anything right."

The crow seemed to nod as it cawed back to him.

"Yeah, you understand. Smart, fella." Burt toiled for the next hour chopping the tree into movable pieces and stacking them by the back gate. Next, he set to work with his pickaxe and shovel, chopping the roots out. One such thrust of the pickaxe struck with a metallic thud.

"Hallo, that sounded funny," remarked Edna coming out with fresh tea.

"Yup, reckon I hit something then," Burt switched to his shovel and began to carefully excavate around the object. After a time, he revealed an old metal box. It used to be painted red, but rust had claimed much of it.

"Well, look at that!" Edna grew wide-eyed with excitement. "Who do you suppose buried that in the garden?"

"I'd bet it was my old grandfather." Burt levered it from the ground. "Father, once told me he hid something out here. I'd quite forgotten until now."

"Why would he do that?" Edna made a grab for the box. "Let me have it. I'll open it and we'll see."

"Hold your horses, dear. Given that this is my granddad's box, I'd rather like to open it myself – if you don't mind!" Burt waved her off and took the box to the patio table. Sitting with his tea, he knocked the rust off the latch and teased it open.

"Well, what's in there?" Edna asked desperate to know.

"I recognise this box. They used to make these for all-butter biscuits. The latches made them great tins to keep." Burt took a breath and swung it open. At once tears flooded his eyes. There on the top, peeking through a waterproof lining bag was a photo of his family. The centre of the scene was his grandfather a World War I veteran. Around him his brothers and sister. Burt's mum and dad who was a veteran in his own right were also present. There were even a few people Burt didn't know.

"That's nice, but why bury a photo? What else is in there?" Edna hurried him.

Burt wouldn't be rushed. He carefully set the photo aside. Beneath were his grandfather's war medals in all their grandeur. "So, that's where they went." Burt lifted some out with shaky hands. He finally had the proof of his grandfather's heroism in World War I.

"Is that all there is?" Edna asked as if dismissing the medals as worthless.

"No." Burt smiled as he laid each medal carefully on the table. Beneath them, he discovered a silver double-hunter pocket watch. There was a pouch of ancient photographs. All taken on a c1912 Vest Pocket Kodak camera that was sitting alongside them in the box. The photos all showed scenes during the war. The final item Burt removed from the box was a pendant on a simple silver chain. The pendant was made from .303 bullet which was likely made for a Lee Enfield bolt action service rifle. "This'll be the bullet which lodged in the insignia badge on my grandfather's beret when he was fighting on the frontline. My father told me he'd kept it as a symbol of good luck as it failed to kill him. I didn't believe him because there was no proof." Burt took a shaky breath. "Now, I'm holding it in my hand."

"And there's me hoping for some treasures. Things to sell and pay off the mortgage, you know." Edna grumbled.

"These are treasures to me, love." Burt smiled. "I don't care about gold or money. These things tell the story of my grandfather. Family and their history are more valuable than anything else in the world. That includes you, Edna."

"You better not be calling me old. I'll belt you one!"
Edna scowled.

"No, Love. I'm saying, you're more valuable to me than
anything else in the world. We've been married for forty
years. I still love you as much as when we first met, Edna."
Burt reached over and hugged her. She might not like the
war memorabilia, but for him, the once-forgotten relics
were a true treasure.

Weltanschauung Magic

Art galleries were supposed to be places of peace and calm. They were supposed to be free of turmoil to allow patrons to enjoy and contemplate the art on show. Weren't they?

Meg approached the window with an artificial spray of eucalyptus and her notebook in her hand. She gazed at life passing by outside and sighed. It was alright for those people in their perfect lives. Meg knew hers was falling apart around her.

It was only 10 a.m. and already she'd had to toss a thief from the gallery, and deal with a debt collector. Worse, her assistant Lizzy had broken a galactic piece called *Weltanschauung*. That was fifteen grand down the drain. Lizzy was waiting for stitches at the hospital having cut herself on Mars.

Meg gave a nod to a familiar passer-by. His smile made her feel better. He always had on a smart blue viscose suit. He could have been her secret admirer going by the number of times he passed the gallery. Of course, he worked nearby and was just passing for coffee, maybe lunch. Yet it was fun to imagine the possibilities.

Meg sighed. Maybe the thief and accident were the day's "yin" and now she could "yang" into the afternoon and enjoy the rest of the day. However, her white blouse was lowering the tone today. The left half was hanging out of her trousers and that would never do.

Tucking her shirt in, she turned from the window and flinched. The man she'd just nodded to stood by the display of elephants, smiling at her.

"Good morning," he began in a rich, deep voice. "I must say, it's always an honour and a blessing to gaze at your beauty every day I pass your gallery.'

Meg blushed and made to speak, but he wasn't done.

"I'm sure nothing for sale in here is as special as you."

"That's high praise, thank you," Meg said through dry lips. She glanced at the door and frowned. "What – er – who are you?"

The man chuckled. "I'm Griffin Grimes and a genuine man; I assure you."

"I'm not falling for your deceit, Mr Grimes. I saw you smiling as you passed the gallery door and window. The security bell did not tinkle either. You..." Meg's words caught in her throat. She choked before forcing herself to say what she was realising. "You didn't come in through the door. How did you get in here?"

"What? Of course, I came through the door. And please call me Griffin."

"You did not – Griffin!" Meg strode over to the door and swung it open. The bell above tinkled gaily, then chimed once again as she shut the door with a thud. "The bell always tinkles and you didn't make it tinkle when you got in here having already passed the door."

"I see you're quite astute." Griffin perched upon an artistically decorated dining chair. "Did you consider—"

Meg pounced. "Get out of that chair! It's worth five thousand pounds and I can't afford your arse to devalue it!"

Griffin acted as if trying to look behind him. "I didn't realise my posterior had such a negative effect on things. I do apologise."

"I'm sorry too. My assistant cost me fifteen grand this morning." Meg turned away as the weight of the situation crushed down upon her. She couldn't afford that loss; she was already struggling to pay the bills.

"Good grief, what did she do? Clean up coffee with a Picasso or something?"

"She dropped the 'Weltanschauung' and smashed it."

"The *Well to shag*, hey. What a shame, sounds erotic," Griffin bounced his eyebrows amorously.

Meg couldn't help but giggle. *"Weltanschauung*. It's German. The word means a comprehensive conception or image of the universe and the human relationship to it. The sculptor Gunter Weiss created a statue of our universe where each planet was a human face."

"Oh, well, that won't help in the bedroom. Sounds ripe for a political debate instead."

"Hmhmm, Yup, and Lizzie smashed Mars, Jupiter and Uranus." Meg flicked her mousey hair from her shoulder and indicated a box containing the remains of the piece."

"Thank goodness, she spared Earth!" Griffin remarked.

"Pardon?"

"Well, if she smashed Earth, we'd all be in the contents of Uranus, wouldn't we?" Griffin laughed.

Meg gave a wry smile. "Very impressive. You just morphed from a smart intelligent gentleman to a silly schoolboy in an expensive suit!"

"Ouch! You sting like a wasp – you know that?" Griffin looked affronted.

"Yes, and I have the memory of an elephant too!" Meg narrowed her eyes at him. "So, let's try again. Who are you and how did you get in here?"

"Would you believe, by magic?"

Meg shook her head.

"May I?" Griffin indicated the spray of eucalyptus.

"Sure." Meg handed it to him.

Griffin held it from the base of the branch. He took a deep breath and ran a hand along the length to the stems of leaves.

Meg gasped in surprise.

The leaves passed between his fingers and re-emerged with red-tinged edges. As the final stem came free of his

164

fingers, a beautiful yellow rosebud unfurled into the most beautiful flower.

"For you," Griffin said with a regal bow.

"That was beautiful!" Meg smelt the rose and smiled. "Thank you."

"Now, you see. With a little magic, one does not need to set a bell chiming when one enters through a regular door." Griffin picked up the box containing the remains of the *Weltanschauung*. He placed it on the counter beside the till.

"What are you doing?" Meg came over tense. The sculptor was already going to murder her without more damage being done to his piece.

Griffin took a shard of Jupiter from the box. The Jovian planet was recognisable by its lines and red spot. Something that made it all the more remarkable was the face of an old man. "I dare say, Lizzie really cracked it when she dropped this one!"

"Ha! You're a real comedian, aren't you?" Meg placed her hands on her hips. "Don't break it anymore, please."

"Trust in me, and you'll be in a world made of fewer pieces," Griffin sang as he took out a large red handkerchief. He laid it over the box, smiled and removed it again. The *Weltanschauung* was gone in place of a large chestnut-brown teddy bear with a red bowtie. "Once again, for you."

Meg took and hugged the bear. "Thank you, but Gunter is coming to collect his piece soon. So, you better make it reappear."

"Of course." Griffin had a swift walk around the gallery. He admired paintings on the walls and paused to look at a few of the sculptures. "Ah, so the piece resided upon this Romanesque inspired pedestal, correct?"

"It did," Meg joined him. "I'll have to find something else to put there now." She reached out to remove the label and flinched as Griffin took and kissed her hand.

165

"Mmm, skin as soft as silk and flavoured with peaches and strawberries," he remarked.

Meg swiftly withdrew her hand. "What, are you going to eat me now?"

"I should say not. I did dine with cannibals once – it was the most inhumane feast imaginable." Griffin shook himself. "Anyway."

"Anyway?" Meg repeated.

Griffin flourished the handkerchief and played it over the marble pedestal.

The material began to take on spherical shapes. Then as it was whisked away, the pedestal was no longer empty.

Meg gasped. The *Weltanschauung* was back in one piece and looking beautiful again. Each of the planets shone as the multicultural faces looked back at her with wisdom that said they contained the vast knowledge of the universe.

"How's that?" Griffin asked.

Meg was turned her shock widened eyes from the valuable piece to Griffin and smiled at him.

"Happy?"

"You just saved my life and my business," she managed as she flung herself on and hugged him.

"Honestly, the pleasure's mine." Griffin grinned and pointed over her shoulder.

Meg turned to see Lizzie standing in the doorway. "Lizzie, you're back. And… Now, you can get in without ringing the bloody bell."

Lizzie was in her early twenties. She had the cutest ginger pigtails, which set off her midnight blue pinafore dress perfectly. "Hi, Meg," she said closing the door so the bell tinkled.

"What the – how in the world?" Meg spluttered.

Lizzie held up a remote control containing just the buttons. "This is how. If we switch the magnet on, it holds the bell so it won't ring." Lizzie demonstrated, then opened the door without a sound. She pressed the second button then closed the door setting the bell tinkling again.

Meg looked between her and Griffin with narrowed eyes. "Which means, Lizzie, you know Griffin and you both set me up."

"We must confess to being in cahoots," Griffin said. "Lizzie told me of your financial difficulties. She explained that she offered to take a pay cut to help you. That you continue to pay her in full while maintaining your kind-heartedness and care for her despite the turmoil and despair you've been going through. I knew then, I had to do something to help. You cannot let the one you've fallen for suffer, can you?"

"So, you had Lizzie break the piece as an excuse for you to sneak in here and magically repair it?" Meg stated while ignoring his last sentence.

"Something like that." Lizzie came over and hugged her boss. "I didn't cut my hand when I dropped the piece this morning. I faked that as an excuse to leave the gallery."

"What did you do?" Meg said in an accusing voice.

Lizzie opened the door again. This time maybe a dozen people entered. All wearing expensive suits and dresses. "I met with lots of wonderful people and brought them here. This is Pierre Domengeaux. He has a cheque for sixteen thousand pounds for the *Weltanschauung*. Everyone else here is an art and sculpture enthusiast. Each is eager to buy and sell pieces here. Griffin owns the art gallery at the Castle Museum; he arranged for everyone to come here today, you see."

"Hello, everyone. Welcome to the Meg-a-lithic art and sculpture gallery and shop. Please come in and take a look around," Meg invited. Turning to Griffin she added, "Thank you so much for helping me."

167

"It's been a pleasure. Although, I did have one request." Griffin said having shaken the rich Frenchman's hand.

"What you have in mind?"

"Will you allow Lizzie to take all these people's money, and come to dinner with me? You see, the rose and the bear weren't just romantic magic. I really do wish to get to know and love you."

Meg took a breath. "Lizzie, you're in charge. Don't bloody well break anything!"

Wendy's Little Miracles

Old Leonard Dyke was a veterinarian. He'd run his clinic in the village for forty years. Some said he should have retired a few years back, but he disagreed. He felt as fit as fiddle, he was still quite able to work and so at seventy-three he was still happily caring for the village's animals.

This particular evening, he was on his way to Celandine Cottage on an urgent call. Smoking away on his pipe, he aimed his beaten old Landrover Discovery along the blackthorn and hawthorn lined country lane. He was excited about this particular call.

On arrival, he was greeted by a volley of barking. Two Old English Sheepdogs bounded to the gate. The enormous black and grey balls of fur were at least twenty-eight-inches high at the withers.

"Bobtail, Go-Go! Nice to see you," Leonard alighted from the car and collected his kit from the back. He approached the gate and made a fuss of the loveable pastoral dogs. He always enjoyed his day when these dogs came to visit his clinic. He knew Bobtail got his name from accidentally docking his tail in a fence as a puppy. Go-Go got his name as he always got into trouble and had to be told to "Go away!"

"Ah, Leonard, glad you could come," said a gentleman coming out to see to the ruckus his dogs were making.

"Wouldn't miss the exciting moment for the world. Adam." Leonard entered the cottage garden causing one of the dogs to trample a patch of marigolds and chrysanthemums, and scare a cockerel into a hasty retreat, in his excitement. "How's Wendy doing?"

"She nested three days ago. About twelve hours ago she started getting restless and panting. She hasn't eaten anything and is now confined to her nest." Adam led the way inside leaving the male dogs in the garden.

"No appearances yet then?" Leonard asked as they walked along oak-panelled hallways and entered the pale orange painted kitchen of teak cabinets and matching table. There beneath the solid furnishing was a great big basket containing the third Old English Sheepdog Wendy. Her swollen belly indicated she was very close to a magical moment.

Adam's wife Gemma and their son and daughter Robert and Mara were watching over her.

"She's not produced yet, no," Adam said.

"Not to worry. We may have a while to wait yet." Leonard put his bag on the sideboard and took out a stethoscope. "Hello, everybody. Exciting night isn't it?" he said with a buoyant smile.

"It really is, Mr, Dyke. We've been waiting all day for Wendy to give us puppies," said Mara looking desperate to touch Wendy the dog but knowing she had to give her room.

"I think we'll have them soon enough," Leonard said. He'd discovered Wendy was pregnant about six weeks ago. The family had noticed she was getting rather chubby and were concerned something was wrong. Since then scans had revealed the truth and today was the birthing day.

"Yes, we will. Would you like some tea, Leonard." Gemma asked.

"I wouldn't say no. Thank you." Leonard knelt by Wendy and smoothed her chin for a moment.

The wise-looking dog gazed at him through friendly brown eyes, took a breath and licked his fingers.

"Good girl, Wendy. You do the work and I'll help where I can, hey?" Leonard placed his stethoscope on her muscular frame in various places. He watched her abdomen contract and nodded. "Oh, yes. She's definitely in labour. "Robert, I need a bowl ready to fill with hot water. Mara, a stack of towels would be most helpful. Can you do that?"

"Yes." Robert left with Mara to get the things at once.

"Any issues?" asked Adam.

"Not as yet… Thanks, Gemma." Leonard rose to sip his tea. "Whatever the case I'm here as long as Wendy needs me."

"We appreciate it," Gemma said as the wait began in earnest.

On the chime of 11 p.m., puppy one was born. Perfectly black and grey just like her mum and tiny considering what she'd become as an adult. Leonard cleaned the amniotic from the puppy's face, causing her to begin squeaking. He pronounced her healthy and placed her with mum.

Wendy nuzzled her with a joyous look on her face. She began licking and caring for at once.

"Aww, look! She's the perfect mother." Gemma said.

"After you anyway," Adam replied and kissed his wife.

"Eww, get a room you two!" Robert chimed in making his sister giggle. He and Mara had been sleeping when puppy one appeared. They were awake and giddy with joy now.

The next three puppies were all males and each arrived healthy by 1 a.m.. By then the children were in bed.

"How are we doing, Doc?" asked Adam stifling a yawn.

"Our x-rays showed six puppies inside Wendy. So, two to go and she's doing great." Leonard gave the wonderful mother a scratch behind the ears.

Puppy five came into the world a 2:23 a.m. and was a surprise. "Wow! She's a chubby little girl. The others will have trouble feeding with her about." Adam remarked.

171

"Indeed, she's a heavy one." Leonard cleaned and checked her like the rest. "She's as fit as a fiddle too," he added allowing the family to meet the large puppy.

"This is amazing!" Gemma beamed having knelt beside Wendy and nestled the puppy with its brothers and sisters.

Wendy received her and began mothering at once. By now her tongue was lolling and didn't look so good.

Leonard could tell she was getting very tired. "You're doing magnificent, girl. One more and then you can relax."

The last puppy didn't appear. After waiting another long hour, Leonard decided to induce with an injection. The puppy came fast after that. He scooped him up and set to work on him with urgency.

"Something wrong?" asked Adam rushing over, looking exhausted himself. He took the puppy in a towel for the veterinarian.

"Thanks. He's stillborn I'm afraid. Can you rub his chest hard for me." Leonard used a tube to suck the puppy's mouth clear of fluid as Adam warmed him with vigorous strokes of the towel.

"Come on, baby. You can survive too!" Gemma begged.

Leonard felt himself sweating as he took the puppy back. He breathed a little air into its tiny lungs. Nothing – he held it upside down and swung it quite quickly back and forth.

"What are you doing?" Adam looked horrified.

"It's okay. I'm using gravity to clear his lungs and—" Leonard heard the puppy cough. He lifted him and listened. Nodding, he resumed the chest massage and then he was beaming as the puppy spluttered into life and began squeaking like it's siblings in the bed with Mum. "Eureka!" Leonard gave mum her last puppy and punched the air in delight.

Adam broke out some whisky and a little celebration was had. What fun Mara and Robert would have, naming the six new puppies in the morning.

What Matters Most

"What's with you, smiling like you won the lottery." Paige curled her arm in her boyfriend Ralph's, nestling against him as they strolled along the beach. Beneath the sultry sun, the relaxing ebb and flow of the warm afternoon tide lapped over their bare toes. The two had been soulmates since the age of twelve. Now twenty-one their affections for one another were just as strong.

"Oh, I did. Only nine years ago, I didn't win money. I won everlasting happiness when I met you." Ralph smoothed his fingers through her long blonde hair as he gave her a little smooch.

"Mmm, thank you, Romeo. So, what's new with you?" Paige picked a pebble and sent it skipping over the waves. She faced him and removed her sunglasses revealing her enchanting sapphire eyes. Despite his happiness today, she felt something was amiss with him. "I know you. What's wrong, sweetheart?"

Ralph shook his head with an adoring grin. "You're so beautiful and smart and—"

"Ralph, please. You must tell me."

"It's nothing. It's just…" Ralph caught her about the waist, leaving her squealing as he lifted and lowered her into the sand.

Paige placed her hands on his cheeks hoping to pull him to face her. She felt his lips close to her navel, his fashionable stubble, tickling as he kissed his way around her belly. She giggled and squirmed but he held her until his loving ritual was done. Only then did he allow her to look into his mahogany eyes. "Finished? Now, talk to me, please," she implored.

Ralph sighed, his hand smoothing her hair. "I'm going to miss you, Paige."

"What?" she took his hands, squeezing with affection as her heart thumped with worry. "What are you saying?"

"My computer company is shutting its Norfolk branch. I have to move to Edinburgh to continue working. I—"

"Ralph…"

"Shush, let me finish."

Paige felt tears welling, but she nodded.

"Thank you." Ralph kissed her. "I know you can't leave the salon. You and your sister are amazing there. I don't ever want you to leave the place you love to work in either."

"But, Ralph…"

"Listen… You stay here and keep the salon rocking. Keep our little home nice for us. I'll go rent a place in Edinburgh for a year. I'll finish my projects and then return to love you again."

The revelation on the beach had been a month ago. Paige hated the idea of letting Ralph go but she knew she had too. He'd worked so hard on his projects; he simply couldn't drop them now.

The last few weeks had gone too fast. Ralph wound up his work and had his paperwork sent to Edinburgh and the new offices while Paige worked with growing sadness in the salon. She and Ralph spent every second they could together. Walking hand-in-hand, taking in movies while sharing popcorn, dining together. Spending all day in bed together on Sunday had been sheer bliss.

Now, like a sledgehammer to the heart – a shattering dream – it was coming to an end. Ralph stood on the platform under the iron stanchions of the train station, with his suitcase stood beside him. He wasn't watching for his train; his eyes were glued to Paige.

She adjusted his lapel and smoothed a stray hair from his shoulder. "You'll be the most handsome man in

Edinburgh, you know. Wear a kilt and take a picture for me."

"I'll make it a priority." Ralph pulled her into a hug. "I may be handsome in Edinburgh, but I won't be happy. I won't be until I travel the six-hundred miles back to you."

The clacking note of an approaching train told of time running short.

"I'll be here waiting for you. You call me every day and I'll make you smile on the video chat, I promise." Paige freed herself, wiping tears from her cheeks. "I'll… miss… you."

"Not more than I'll miss you, sweetheart." Ralph watched his train stop and disgorge its passengers onto the platform. He embraced Paige again, drawing in her sweet, floral perfume. "Stay safe and keep smiling for me, okay?"

Paige couldn't help a sob leaving her body. "I'll do my best, handsome. Now, go get 'em." She kissed him one final time and then stepped away. "Go on, before I handcuff and drag you home again."

"Don't tempt me." Ralph smiled and winked, then he was walking down the platform with his case in hand.

Paige swayed on the balls of her feet as she watched him enter the train. She held her ponytail and hugged herself; not knowing if or when she'd ever feel Ralph hugging her again. As she did, she felt something new about her neck. Taking the gold chain in hand she found herself holding a small ruby heart. On the back, it read *Hold my heart until I return – Love eternally Ralph.* "What a slushy Romeo," she said to herself with a tearful smile. She realised Ralph must have slipped it on when he hugged her last.

Paige couldn't see him on the train but she waved as it left. Then with a sadness lying heavy on her heart, she walked away from the platform. The bustling coffee shops, newsagent and bakery were lost to her. He'd been gone for seconds; she was already missing him.

Her phone was ringing in her bag.

"Ugh, not now!" she groaned while digging it out from between her hairbrush and antiperspirant. Not looking at the screen, she answered it with an annoyed flick. "Yeah, Paige speaking…"

"Turn around."

"Ralph?" Paige felt her heart flutter in her chest. She faced the platform and there with his phone to his ear was Ralph.

He beamed and waved to her.

Paige almost dropped her phone. Her eyes flooding with joy, she ran through the crowds to him.

Ralph threw open his arms and caught her with a deep sigh of relief.

"Sweetheart, you should be on the train to Edinburgh." Paige freed herself and kissed him in a moment of pure euphoria. "Why are you here?"

"I'd just sat down on the train when I received an answer to an email I sent to my boss on Thursday." Ralph grinned. "Now, I'm not going to Edinburgh anymore."

"I don't understand. You didn't quit, did you?" Paige wiped her eyes, her hand shaking as she took his.

"No," Ralph smoothed his hand over her cheek. "I'm going to be working from home with you by my side from now on."

"That's fantastic! But how?" Paige felt herself tingling all over – she couldn't believe it.

"I told my boss his pay rise meant nothing to me and neither did a nice new office with views over a castle. I realised none of it matters if you're unhappy. I told him if I can't be with and love you every day my ability to work would fade away. He agreed and just this morning made the arrangements for me to stay."

"I don't believe it. You gave up so much money for me." Paige put her head on his chest.

"I did – I don't need it. You see, you were my lottery win nine years ago. So, long as I have you, my precious, Paige – I'll be the richest man in the world.

Paige broke into a beautiful smile. "I love you, Ralph." She knew then as they left the station, she wouldn't stop smiling for the longest time to come.

About the author

Author Mason Bushell, is a naturalist, chef and writer from Norfolk in the UK. He loves nothing more than to write among the trees, near his home.

He is an avid short story writer and is always working with his characters unless Lucy Dog steals his laptop for a walkies!

Like to Read More Work Like This?

Then sign up to our mailing list and download our free collection of short stories, *Magnetism*. Sign up now to receive this free e-book and also to find out about all of our new publications and offers.

Sign up here:
  http://eepurl.com/gbpdVz

Please Leave a Review

Reviews are so important to writers. Please take the time to review this book. A couple of lines is fine.

Reviews help the book to become more visible to buyers. Retailers will promote books with multiple reviews.

This in turn helps us to sell more books... And then we can afford to publish more books like this one.

Leaving a review is very easy.

Go to https://bit.ly/43WzDQS, scroll down the left-hand side of the Amazon page and click on the "Write a customer review" button.

Other Writing by Mason Bushell

The Jinn

At just five-inches tall, he's a demon with attitude, and he is fed-up with people summoning him through his talisman. With sass and cheek aplenty, he wanders grumpily through a saga of adventures. He meets learner drivers, babies, and zoo creatures, to name but a few, each in need of his special brand of help.

"Mason Bushell has created an amusing little character in the Jinn & you can't help but smile at his antics & the way he expresses himself. If you are looking for a quick fast read that will leave you with a smile, give it a read." (*Amazon*)

Order from Amazon:

Paperback: ISBN 978-1-910542-62-0
eBook: ISBN 978-1-910542-63-7

Other Publications by Bridge House

The Day Chuck Berry Died
by Ian Inglis

A collection of eclectic and original short stories that bring into
focus those decisive moments in a person's life whose
significance may not be recognised at the time, but which often
have profound and lasting impacts long into the future.

The distorted contours of human nature, as practised in the
daily activities of professional footballers; the repercussions of
a young man's visit to the battlefields of Flanders to visit his
grandfather's grave; a surprising encounter in a Parisian cafe.
Choices made on the basis of what we know – or what we
think we know – which come back to torment us, challenge us,
enlighten us; attitudes and behaviour we can barely
comprehend; routine events and situations that bring with them
periods of great sadness or unexpected happiness; confusion
and clarity when long-hidden truths are finally revealed.

Order from Amazon:

Paperback: ISBN 978-1-914199-32-5
eBook: ISBN 978-1-914199-33-2

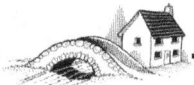

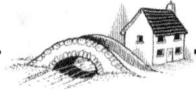

I Knew it in the Bath
by Linda Flynn

I Knew it in the Bath is a collection of absorbing short stories
which show that no matter how we expect events to unfold, life
has a way of confounding us. What will a woman do to save
her friend? Do we really know when we're being watched?
Why did Dora throw the iron through the window? What's the
best way to take revenge on a cheating partner?

Settle back for an engaging read through these humorous,
sinister and thought-provoking stories, but try not to drop your
book in the bath!

Linda Flynn, a frequent contributor to our annual themed
anthologies, gives us food for thought in the stories collected
in *I Knew in in the Bath.*

"I can't recommend this anthology enough. Linda Flynn has
such a way with words." (*Amazon*)

Order from Amazon:

Paperback: ISBN 978-1-914199-28-8
eBook: ISBN 978-1-914199-29-5

www.ingramcontent.com/pod-product-compliance
Lightning Source LLC
Chambersburg PA
CBHW051514170626
46811CB00002B/817